FRIDAY EVENING

'You're being petty now,' Ethan Riley cried as he drove along High Lane.

'I don't think I am,' Katie Frost snapped. 'You're the one who accused me of all sorts. Can't you see how embarrassing it was?'

Katie had been having a great evening until half an hour ago. She and Ethan had been out at an eighteenth birthday party. Tommy Mason, one of Katie's friends, had been talking to her while Ethan was at the bar fetching drinks. She hadn't given him the come-on, they'd been mates for years, yet Ethan took the hump with her.

'You made me look a fool, like you didn't trust me,' she added, holding onto the door handle when he rounded a corner a tad too fast.

'It wasn't you I didn't trust. He was way too close for my liking.'

'I've known him since we were five! He's a friend, and that's all.'

'Well, it didn't seem that way to me.'

She glared at him, exasperated. 'Stop the car.'

'Don't be daft. We're nearly there.'

'I'd rather walk for a few minutes than stay with you for one second longer.'

'Fine.' He pulled sharply into the kerb.

'You are such a baby at times.'

Ethan calmed down, enough to apologise. 'I just saw him with you and I... I got a bit jealous, that's all.'

'A bit?' She raised her eyebrows.

He threw her the smile that usually melted her heart. It didn't work this time, so he tried the next best thing.

'Do you fancy a kebab? My treat?'

She groaned loudly and shook her head. 'You can stick your kebab where the sun doesn't shine.'

'Don't be like that. Come on, Katie!'

She got out, slamming the car door in temper, and marched away. When the vehicle screeched off noisily, she gave Ethan the finger and thrust her hands into her coat pockets.

Two minutes later, she was regretting her impulsive actions. It was half past eleven. She hadn't planned on coming home that evening. But after that accusation, there was no way she was going back to stay at Ethan's house, not even with all its luxuries.

The night was nippy for late February, a gentle breeze blowing through the trees ahead. She wrapped her arms across her chest, feeling sorry for herself, and a little bit stupid. She and Ethan often argued like this. He was quite a hothead, but Katie knew he'd be sorry tomorrow when he'd calmed down. She wasn't at fault. It was him who'd over-reacted.

She crossed over the road to the back of Carlisle Street and along by the row of terraced properties towards her house. A yawn engulfed her, bed beckoning. She couldn't wait to get home now. Perhaps her mum might be up, and she could have a moan at her.

But then she heard loud voices. It sounded like an argument. Seeing two people in front of her, she dipped behind a tree so she wouldn't be seen. She listened intently, covering her mouth with her hand to stop herself from interrupting.

Surely that couldn't be right.

She heard a gate open and close and chanced another peek. He was still there. Curious to know why, she came out of her hiding place.

'Oi,' she shouted. 'I want a word with you.'

SATURDAY - DAY ONE

CHAPTER ONE

Detective Inspector Allie Shenton was exhausted. After a restless night's sleep, she relished the silence before she had to get out of bed. She and her team had been out the night before. A meal had turned into a drinking session, and her head was pounding.

It had been a great evening, well, week, of celebrations for her fiftieth birthday. She hated to say it, but she seemed to be getting too old to cope with three nights out on the trot. Gone were the days where she could stroll in at three a.m. and be as bright as a button when she got up a couple of hours later.

She felt something wet on the side of her face and opened her eyes. Her dog, Dexter, was staring at her.

'What do you want?' she muttered, stroking his head and smiling as his tail thumped a greeting on the duvet.

Poppy, her foster daughter, appeared in the doorway, carrying a mug. 'You look like you need a cuppa.' She put the drink on the bedside table.

'Lifesaver. What time is it?'

'Just gone eight.'

Allie still didn't move.

'Did you have a good night?' Poppy asked.

'Mm-hmm.' Allie yawned.

'What time did you get in?'

'I have no idea.'

'Dirty stop out.'

Allie rolled over, stretching out her limbs. She placed a hand behind the back of her head. Another yawn.

'I'll get a shower and come down to you,' she said, hoping Poppy didn't want to talk to her until she was fully awake. She was a sweet thing, but at this time of morning, her incessant chatter felt too much.

Her mobile rang, and she reached for it. It was Perry, her detective sergeant.

'Morning,' she said. 'How's your head?'

'A bit iffy. You?'

'It doesn't feel like my own. It was a great night, though.'

'Are you still in bed?'

'Mind your own business,' she joked.

'A young woman's body has been found, about half an hour ago,' he told her.

And just like that, Allie was alert. She sat up quickly. 'Where?'

'Over by the pond at the back of High Lane and Park Avenue.'

'Have you rung the others?'

'About to do it now.'

'I'll be there ASAP.'

Allie rushed into the bathroom, ignoring her headache in an instant. It was nothing that two painkillers couldn't mask. But, halfway through her shower, she remembered she'd promised Poppy a day's shopping in Manchester. Someone was going to be in bad books.

When she went downstairs, she was dressed in a navy

trouser suit, a white shirt open at the neck, and flat lace-up boots. She had a feeling she'd be on her feet for most of the day, so comfort was an issue. Her long dark hair was damp, but she'd tied it back out of the way, drying only her fringe for quickness.

Poppy was sitting in the kitchen with Allie's husband, Mark. He stared at Allie and sighed dramatically.

'You've been called into work, haven't you?'

'I have, sorry. Something has come in this morning.'

'A murder?' Poppy's tone was inquisitive.

'I won't really know until I get there.' Allie hated talking details with her family. 'Will you two be okay without me? I'm so sorry—'

'Allie, it's your job,' Mark said and added another sigh.

'I know, I know, but we had big plans for today.' Allie paused, looking at Poppy. 'You're not too upset about Manchester?'

'Yes, but we could do it next weekend, or later if you're still busy.'

Allie grinned at her. 'Great. I was really excited to go, though.'

'Me, too.'

Poppy's nose was now in her phone. Allie reckoned she'd be texting her friend.

'Maybe Victoria might like to come over for the day?'

'Yeah, that would be cool.'

Mark mouthed a silent thank you. Allie knew he'd be grateful of the time to sit and watch the footie on TV that afternoon. She searched out her keys, kissed him on the forehead and was on her way. So much for a relaxing weekend.

High Lane was in the north of the city, a long road that went from Smallthorne to Chell. She drove along it and turned off at Haywood Hospital. Left again led her into Park Avenue. It sounded a grand place, but in essence was a row of forty terraced houses whose rear yards on the right backed onto a wide cobblestoned path and straight onto an open field. It was often used as a cut-through to the Bennett Estate, several streets of privately owned houses amid the many rented.

It was half past eight when Allie got there to find the scene alive with officers and emergency vehicles. A cordon had already been placed across the crime scene area, and she could see a tent erected. She parked as close as she could, then showed her warrant card to the scene officer, who logged her in as attending.

She dipped under the crime scene tape. To the right, she spotted two other members of her team, Perry, who she'd spoken to earlier, and DC Frankie Higgins, huddled together in conversation. DC Sam Markham, she knew, would already be on her way to the station.

They turned as she approached.

'Morning boss, how're you feeling?' Frankie asked with a wide grin, his face popping out from the hood of a forensic suit.

'Let's say I'm glad of a bit of winter sun so I can wear my shades,' Allie replied.

'Well, you would insist on getting two more rounds of drinks in.' He shook his head. 'You know us young ones can take it much better than you old folk.'

'*I* wasn't the one who was dancing in the street after we left.'

'I tried my best to get you to join us. But you weren't steady enough on your feet.'

'I was not drunk,' Allie protested weakly. 'I was tipsy.'

Perry handed a suit to Allie. 'It was a terrific night, though. Did you get home okay?'

'Yes, thanks. I was woken rudely by someone slobbering on my face.'

'Was Mark being a naughty boy?' Perry asked in mock-innocence.

Allie snorted; that was quite funny. 'It was Dexter, if you must know.' Dexter was a four-year-old fell terrier they had rehomed last year. Mark had wanted a dog for ages, and when Poppy had come to stay, Allie had been persuaded to take on a rescue.

A movement to their right had them all turning their heads. Dave Barnett, the senior CSI, came out of the crime scene tent.

Allie ripped open the covering for the forensic suit and pulled it out. 'Joking aside, it's time to get this show on the road. Who found her?'

'A woman going to work this morning. She lives three streets away, Douglas Close.' Perry pointed behind.

'Did she say if she knew the victim?'

'She didn't,' Frankie told her. 'Know her, that is.'

'Okay, then, let's crack on.' Allie nodded. 'We need to find out what happened to this poor girl.'

CHAPTER TWO

With her forensic gear now on, Allie made her way over to Dave. She scanned the surroundings while she walked. The path off where the body had been found led to a large pond, manmade and set in a small woodland. A group of onlookers were already rubbernecking at the edge of the cordon.

Allie wondered if whoever had killed the young woman knew the area, choosing this particular place because it was easy to conceal a body. Or maybe it was a random attack, an act of rage, someone in the wrong place at the wrong time. The email she'd received from Dave about the first details mentioned there was blood on the gravel path she'd been found near to. Allie hoped she hadn't been dragged but knew it was more than likely. Humans could be such nasty creatures at times.

She marched on, taking deep breaths and bracing herself for what was to come. Perry had told her the woman seemed to be no older than mid-teens. The thought of seeing a body similar size to Poppy's was already giving her palpitations. Like Poppy, their victim would have been at the start of her life. Tears stung Allie's eyes, and she blinked them away. Luckily, her team knew that when she saw the worst in people, she never bowed down to hiding her emotions.

Dave saw her approaching, removed his mask. 'Hey, Allie, how's the head?'

'It's been much better,' she admitted as she drew level with him. 'How about you? Please tell me you have a hangover, too.'

'A little bit of one. It was a great night, though.'

'So everyone says. What have you got for me?' she wanted to know.

'Female, approximate age sixteen to nineteen, although may possibly be younger. I'll leave that for Chris to ascertain.' Christian Longhorn was the pathologist on call.

'Any ID?'

'Not that I can see on or near the body. No phone or handbag either.'

'Maybe the search team will find those. Let's hope they didn't get thrown into the water. Any signs of a struggle?'

'None. I think that's because of the trauma to the back of the head. She was struck twice, once across the face, which may have caused her to lose her balance and then fall backwards and hit her head heavily as she landed.'

'Fell or pushed?'

'Not sure yet. She caught the edging stone on her way down. There's blood on it. She'd have been dead in minutes if not straightaway, poor lamb.'

A rush of nausea rolled through Allie, and it wasn't anything to do with her hangover. She took a deep breath to quell it.

'Anything else?' she asked when she'd composed herself again.

'She has a shoe that came off and has been retrieved, and

the skin on the side of the relevant foot is grazed. I know this isn't the crime scene, and I'm assuming she died nearer to the backs of the houses in Park Avenue and was then dragged out of sight. I expect we might see a trail of blood spots when it gets lighter.'

'Sexually motivated, do you think?'

'Hard to say, but her clothes are intact so, either not, or the suspect was disturbed.'

Allie grimaced at the images that were flooding her mind. Murder investigations were bad enough, but when their victims were young, it became doubly hard to keep emotions at bay.

'Do you think it was a robbery gone wrong?' she queried next. 'Maybe she fought too much, and someone saw red. It would explain why there are no personal belongings close by.'

'I'll let you know more once we've done our job.'

'Okay, I'll leave you to it for now.' She stared at him meaningfully. 'You owe me a night out, a quiet one. You said life begins at fifty, and this is not what I had in mind.'

They shared a smile before shouts interrupted them.

'Boss!' Frankie ran towards them, his hand in the air carrying an evidence bag. 'We have an ID card. It was found close to the path.'

'Ah, that's a start,' Allie said. 'At least we can break the grim news to the family and—'

Frankie pointed to the row of houses behind. 'She lives in Park Avenue, number six. I can see the gate from here, so her next of kin could turn up at any moment.'

Allie closed her eyes momentarily, letting the news sink in. For the second time that day, she almost felt the blood draining from her body. If they didn't move quickly, someone might see more than they had anticipated. She'd hate anyone to find out a loved one had been killed from hearsay or looking on.

She ripped off her forensic suit, struggling to get out of it quickly enough. 'Come with me, Frankie. I'll get Perry back to hold the fort until I return. We have to tell our victim's family before they spot what's going on. I can't imagine how they'll feel knowing she was minutes away from home.'

CHAPTER THREE

Donna Frost yawned as she stood in front of the kitchen window, waiting for the kettle to boil. It had been two years since her husband, Max, had died, and even now she missed him as if it were yesterday that he'd been taken from them.

Their marriage had been tumultuous, though, to say the least. They'd always been bickering at one another. She would always be nagging, he said. *She* would always be worrying, she'd tell him.

The kettle boiled, and she threw teabags into two mugs, quickly topping them up with hot water.

The kitchen door opened, and in waddled her daughter, Shona. She was seven months pregnant, and her boyfriend had moved into the front bedroom with her two months ago. There was no way they could afford to rent anywhere with the extortionate prices of everything nowadays, so Donna had suggested they share Shona's room. One more mouth to feed wouldn't be any hardship, and Jacob gave her money each week towards the bills.

A baby was going to be expensive, but what a joy it would be. Donna was so pleased she was going to be a nan and only wished Max would have been here to see the next generation of their family being born.

It had been a bit of a shock at first, with Shona being twenty-one and only with her boyfriend for a year when she got caught. Mind, at nineteen Donna had been pregnant herself with Shona. Three years later, Nate had come along, and then finally, Katie twelve months on. It had been mayhem when they were little, but they'd been amazing since Max had died, growing really close.

Max had good friends, too, who looked after her as well as the family. But she still had needs, and her skin reddened as she thought of what she'd been doing a couple of nights ago. She'd finished her shift behind the bar at The Fox and Hare, when a car had drawn up alongside her. She'd been seeing Woody for three months now, in secret. They'd gone for a drive in the car before he'd dropped her off at home.

She sighed when she thought of their last conversation. He was wanting more than she was willing to give. Woody had been Max's friend, too. It didn't bode well if anyone found out they were seeing each other. The fallout was going to be horrendous when the time was right, and she wasn't ready for it.

'I can't wait to get this big lump out of my body once and for all,' Shona said, pulling out a chair at the table. She lowered herself carefully down with a huge sigh. 'She's kept me awake for most of the night.'

'You should relish the peace and quiet before she does arrive.' Donna joined her, and placed one of the mugs in front of her daughter.

'It's exhausting, isn't it? I don't know how you managed to do it three times. Will it really hurt so much?'

Donna smiled. 'Of course it will. But you'll forget all the pain as soon as she's in your arms. Then you'll get the pelt of love that means you'll take care of her, no matter what, for the rest of your life.'

'Aw. Did you get that when I was born?'

'You're having a laugh, aren't you?' Donna sniggered. 'You were such a huge baby I was in labour for two days, and I was definitely glad to see the back of you once you were out.'

Shona pouted. 'You are a terrible mother.'

Donna eyed her firstborn with adoration. Her kids were her world, and she would do anything for them. Shona and her sister, Katie, were so much alike in looks and mannerisms. Both had long blonde hair, big blue eyes and button noses: both had tempers that had got them into several fights with each other over the years. As for Donna, apart from the many wrinkles, the grey coming through her roots that she dyed every four weeks, and the extra spare tyre around her middle, she wasn't ageing that badly.

There was a noise behind them, and her son, Nate, sauntered into the room, wearing pyjamas bottoms, an oversized jumper, and thick socks.

'Morning,' he mumbled, scratching his head.

'Morning, love. There's tea in, if you boil the kettle, dunk a teabag, and add milk and sugar to a mug.'

'Ha ha.' Nate smirked. 'I suppose you both want another.'

'Ooh, that would be grand, ta.' Donna grinned at him.

Shona was scrolling through her phone and stopped to read something. 'There's a police car blocking off the backs. It's all over Facebook.' She enlarged the photo and peered closer. 'I can see one of those white tents over by the woods.'

Donna rolled her eyes. 'It's probably the Gallagher family. I bet they've been scrapping again.'

'But that wouldn't—'

'Let me see.' Nate came to stand next to her.

There was a knock on the front door. Donna went through to the hall.

'I bet this will be Hannah coming along to tell us the gossip. She never misses a trick, and I know she'll—' Donna opened the door to find a woman about her age with dark hair tied back from her face, and a man in is twenties wearing a black woollen hat standing on the pavement. Both had suits underneath thick padded coats, and solemn faces.

Something dropped inside her stomach.

'Morning. Mrs Frost?' the woman said.

'Yes.' Donna cleared her throat as her words got stuck. 'Yes, can I help you?'

The woman held up her warrant card. 'I'm Detective Inspector Allie Shenton, and this is my colleague, Detective Constable Frankie Higgins. May we come in for a moment, please?'

CHAPTER FOUR

Allie loved and hated the first few hours of a murder investigation in equal measure. She was always the bearer of bad news, trying not to let the victim's family's pain seep under her skin, and she had to view everyone as a suspect until either she had the information to charge someone with the crime, or evidence eliminated them from enquiries.

It often made her feel sneaky, trying to coax out things that perhaps people wouldn't want her to know. But her job was one of investigating, getting to the bottom of things. With a sympathetic mannerism, she could handle anything.

Once inside the property, she and Frankie walked along a narrow hallway, stairs at the end of it to the first floor. As they did so, her gaze fell upon photo after photo of who she assumed would be family members. There was a large one of a man sitting astride a motorbike, and a wedding photo of a couple in the nineties. Children wise, there appeared to be two girls and a boy, throughout the years. Allie swallowed when she came to a row of school photographs. The last one was definitely the girl in the field behind.

Mrs Frost showed her into a kitchen where a heavily

pregnant woman was standing with her back against the worktop in front of the window, a tense look on her face. Katie's older sister, she surmised, and the other girl in the family portraits.

The kitchen was dated but clean, a large table taking over the centre of it. Allie smelt toast in the air; saw two empty mugs on the drainer.

Breaking the news was the hardest part. The frowns, the disbelief, then the grief sinking in when it all became real. Allie urged everyone to sit at the table before one of them collapsed.

'I'm so sorry to tell you that a body has been found on the grassed area behind your property, and we believe it to be your daughter, Katie.'

'What?' Donna shook her head. 'It can't be. She's over at Ethan's house and...'

'I'm so sorry.' Allie waited for the initial burst of emotions to subside before continuing. 'May I take your first names?' she asked then, wanting to build a rapport straightaway.

'I'm Donna, and this is my daughter, Shona,' the eldest woman said between sobs. She appeared to be in her late thirties, with short blonde-greying hair and would be extremely pretty when she got around to smiling again. 'This is my son, Nate.'

The young girl sobbing in her arms clung on to her mum, shock clear in her eyes. The lad was trying desperately not to crack, but his focus was on the wall behind.

'Are there only the three of you?' Allie asked gently, aware of the people in the photos.

'Yes, there is now. Well, and Jacob, Shona's partner.' Donna wiped at her eyes.

Allie's thoughts returned to the man in the photographs, wondering if he'd left of his own accord or was now deceased. She hoped there would be someone to comfort Donna, as she could sense as a mum she would look after her family before herself.

'We're all really close,' Shona whispered. 'Especially since Dad died.'

Ah, she was probably right.

'It was two years ago,' Donna explained. 'Bowel cancer. He barely had any warning, but his whole body was riddled with it when he found out and he was gone three months later.'

'I'm so sorry for your loss.' Allie meant it. Hearing how Katie was murdered was going to be doubly hard after such a tragedy. With a deep breath, she went through everything she knew so far. There were tears from them all, the disbelief setting in.

'How could someone do that to my beautiful daughter?' Donna cried. 'She never did anyone any harm.'

'Do you know where Katie was last night?' Allie wanted to know.

'She was with her boyfriend, Ethan Riley. They were going to a party, at the Bennett Cricket Club. She was supposed to be staying with him overnight, that's why I didn't think to check where she was this morning.'

'Would she usually check in on her phone? Perhaps via a message?'

'No, we're not really into that. Well, she is – was. Katie's phone went everywhere with her.'

'She would message me a lot,' Shona said, for the first time joining in with the conversation. 'But not when she was out with Ethan.'

'What is he like?'

'Nice, thinks the world of her,' Donna said. 'Although I'm not sure what happened last night. I wonder why she was coming home.'

Allie remained silent, hoping Donna might elaborate on things. But she stayed quiet. It was perhaps a good sign.

'How long have they been together?' she went on.

'Six, seven months.' Donna sniffed. 'She stayed over most weekends. He has a bigger home than us.'

'His parents are loaded,' Shona explained, with more than a hint of envy.

'Do you all get on with him?'

'Yes, he's nice.' Donna nodded.

'And you, Nate. Did you get on well with Ethan?' He'd said nothing yet, and she wanted to bring him into the conversation if she could.

Nate shrugged. 'Yeah, he was okay.'

Donna sat forward with a frown. 'You don't think he'd do this to Katie, do you?'

CHAPTER FIVE

'We have to explore every possibility, Donna,' Allie soothed. 'It's standard procedure, but it doesn't mean we suspect anyone.'

'Ethan loved her,' Shona said. 'I thought she was so lucky to have him. I wish Jacob was like that.'

'Your partner?' Allie probed, recalling the name from earlier.

Shona nodded, wiping away more tears that had fallen. She looked at Donna. 'Mum, I don't think I can tell him. I can't tell anyone. It's… it's…'

'I'll do it, love,' Donna comforted her.

Allie saw before her a strong woman. Donna seemed to be keeping her own grief at bay for her family. No doubt later, when things had sunk in, and their family became the centre of the news, she would perhaps shed tears.

Allie couldn't begin to think about that. Poppy would be getting extra hugs when she next saw her, that was for sure.

'I do have to ask some awkward questions now,' she went on. 'Is there anyone you think who may have wanted to harm

Katie? Has she mentioned anything to you that she was worried about?'

The Frost family glanced at each other, searching for clues among themselves, but in the end they all shook their heads.

'Did Katie go to work, or further education?'

'She was at Staffordshire College, studying business studies.' Donna half-smiled. 'She wanted to open her own business one day, but she never could make up her mind what to do. One minute she was going to be a florist, the next own a bookshop. Then she wanted a coffee shop. She was a dreamer.'

Nate pinched the bridge of his nose and dropped his head. Donna reached out a hand and covered his. He grasped it tightly, a sob emerging.

Allie glanced at Frankie. It was time to leave. She had said all she could for now. They needed time on their own to digest what had happened. But first she had one more thing to do.

'It might be helpful for me to see Katie's room,' she said. 'I promise to be respectful, but it's also important for me and my team to get an insight as to what Katie was like.'

'That's private,' Nate protested.

'It needs to be done, son.' Donna told him. 'We have to catch the... bastard who did this to her.' She turned to Allie. 'It's the second door on the right upstairs, through the first room. Would you like me to come with you?'

'No, it's fine.' Allie nodded her thanks and left the family with Frankie, knowing that her detective constable would be mindful they were grieving.

Katie's bedroom appeared to be the smallest. It had barely room for the single bed, wardrobe, and chest of drawers that were crammed into it. But what Allie saw was a girl who liked her sparkle.

She sat down on the end of the bed, glancing around.

Katie seemed to have been happy here, she could tell. There was a nice vibe to her surroundings, and even with the grief settled on the house, it still seemed a warm place.

Which beggared belief that something so nasty could happen to her. It was time to find her backstory. Allie's job was to work out whether Katie had been attacked by a stranger, or if it was someone she knew. And to do it in the most sensitive manner.

Just then she spotted a familiar emblem on a tote bag. It was from the local boxing club. She reached for it but, before she could take a closer look, there was a commotion downstairs, a voice shouting along the hallway.

Allie went down to rejoin them. In the kitchen, Shona was being comforted by a man she confirmed to be Jacob.

'I'm so sorry for your loss,' she said to him after introducing herself. 'But while I have you all present now, I need to ask about your whereabouts.'

'Why's that?'

Jacob's tone was defensive, his glances at Nate raising Allie's suspicions.

'Routine, nothing more. We have to ask everyone who has seen Katie over the past week or so, to build up a picture of what was going on in her life. Where were you all last night?'

'I was at work until eleven,' Donna said, her gaze flitting around the room. 'At the pub a few streets down, The Hare and Hound. I work there five nights a week.'

'I was in bed by nine,' Shona said. 'I was watching TV.'

Allie's eyes went next to Nate and Jacob who were both avoiding her. Something was off. 'Nate?' she questioned first.

'Me and Jacob went to a party at the cricket club for a couple of pints. We were back here about eleven.'

'Yeah, that's right,' Jacob concurred.

'He was in bed not long after,' Shona replied. 'He woke me up.'

'What time was that?'

'Quarter to midnight?'

'Which cricket club?'

'The Bennett.'

Allie glanced at Frankie to see he was busy noting it down. An unease had dropped on the room, and she was struggling to work out why.

'Okay, we'll leave you for now. There will be a family liaison officer assigned to you shortly, and also a police presence for the next few days. If you're able to identify Katie's body later this evening, we can do that. Or we can wait until the morning, it's entirely up to you and how you feel. A postmortem will take place this afternoon.'

'Where will she be?' Donna asked.

'At the mortuary.' Allie raised a hand before they could protest. 'I'm sorry that a postmortem is necessary. I know that's upsetting, but it's imperative, too. It will establish the cause of Katie's death and help us find who took her from you. I'm waiting on confirmation that everything is ready for you.'

'I don't want to see her, Mum.' Shona shook her head vehemently.

'You don't need to, love,' Donna said. 'I'll do it.'

'I'll come with you,' Jacob offered.

'No, it's fine if you—'

'I'd like to.'

Donna nodded her thanks.

'I can arrange for first thing in the morning,' Allie decided. 'There's no rush at all. Is there anything you'd like to ask, or know, before we go? Donna?'

'No, I want to be alone with my family.'

Allie handed her a contact card. 'Please call if you need me, but also don't be afraid to chat with any of the officers who will be around.' She paused. 'You obviously won't be able to visit the crime scene yet until we've finished gathering our evidence, but I also think it's best that you stay away from the area for now. It's so close to home that I don't want you to have lingering memories of what we will be doing as part of the investigation. I'll come and see you this evening to give you an update.'

Allie left then, Frankie closing the door behind them. Outside on the street, uniformed officers were going house-to-house. There were two liveried police vehicles parked up together, and no doubt a few more at the back. A mobile police base would be set up for the operation, and the cordon widened soon to take in anything they might find.

'That was awful,' Frankie said, followed by a huge sigh.

'It really was,' Allie agreed. 'Thanks for keeping quiet in there. Did they say anything of interest when I went upstairs?'

'Nothing I caught, but something I saw. There was a membership card on the worktop for Kennedy's Boxing Club. I couldn't quite see whose it was, though.'

'Interesting. We'll follow that up later. Because I found a tote bag with the company logo in Katie's room.'

CHAPTER SIX

Allie and Frankie made their way back to the crime scene. News was obviously getting out, no doubt due to teenagers sharing news on the socials, even if they didn't have a definitive name yet.

There were an abundance of people around the cordon now. Three teenagers on pushbikes all stopped in a row were pointing in the distance. Several people in ones and twos were chatting or observing. A couple with four dogs running rings around their feet.

The day had lightened up a little, so more people were out on their daily business. Grey-black clouds were fading in the distance, and Allie was glad to see they were going rather than coming to rain down on their crime scene.

She felt the need to find out more about Katie, so put a call through to Sam.

'Morning, Sam. Sorry to ruin your weekend,' Allie greeted.

'It is what it is. How are things there?'

'We've learned that our victim is named Katie Frost. She's seventeen and lives in the street that directly backs on to the area she was found.'

'Really?' There was shock in Sam's tone. 'How awful. So they can see everything?'

'Not quite, but it is extremely close. It's going to haunt them for the rest of their lives.'

'Maybe it will become a comfort to them once this is all settled.'

'Perhaps. I need you to check out the usual stuff on social media, please. Katie had an active Facebook and WhatsApp presence, a little bit on Instagram and TikTok, too, so can you start with those? Also, monitor them for me to see what happens during the day?'

'Will do. I've started the murder wall in readiness.'

Sam was referring to their various boards that would hold the information as it came in. They had a digital board nowadays, but they also used an old-school whiteboard as well as a cork board.

Leaving that part of the investigation in Sam's capable hands, Allie finished the call and spoke to Frankie.

'Can you check in with the uniformed officers, see if they've picked up anything straightaway and then let me know anything of interest?'

Frankie nodded, and they went their separate ways.

While she walked back to join the others, Allie kept her eyes peeled, but it all seemed pretty normal. Well, apart from a massive police presence, that would no doubt be joined by the press shortly, if they weren't already there.

She rounded the corner back onto the field and spotted Perry chatting to their DCI, Jenny Brindley.

'How's the head faring?' Jenny queried as she reached them.

She was wrapped up for blizzard conditions, her pink bobble hat seeming out of place alongside her black coat, scarf, suit, and boots. But Allie didn't blame her for keeping warm. There was certainly a nip in the air for the time of year.

'It's kind of being forgotten for now, ma'am.' Allie gave a half-smile. 'I've visited the family. Mother, older brother, and sister who has a live-in boyfriend, Jacob. We're checking them all out at the moment. Shona is twenty-one, Jacob twenty-two, and Nate eighteen. Dad deceased two years previous. Katie was going out with a lad called Ethan Riley.'

Jenny looked at Perry. 'Did you get anything from the witness who found her?'

'Not really. She was in a terrible state, barely a woman herself.'

'It's never nice to find.'

'I'm heading over to talk to Ethan now,' Allie told her. 'I'll take Perry with me.' She shook her head. 'So close to home could mean it's someone lashing out on impulse. I'm not sure this isn't premeditated with only one wound and an attempt to hide the body, albeit a silly one.'

'Someone could have followed her here, took a chance as she reached the path before she disappeared inside,' Jenny said. 'The likelihood of it being a stranger is quite low until we have more details. I'm going back to the station as you seem to have it all under control.'

Allie nodded. They all knew the drill, what to do next, and again, after that. It was ingrained procedure that happened with every murder case. It never made the job easy, but at least there was routine to it.

And routine was where most people slipped up.

A hand waving in the distance caught her eye. It was Simon Cole, senior crime reporter for *Stoke News*. She waved and walked over to him. She and Simon went back years, a mutual respect of each other's jobs, and now they had someone else in common. Simon had married Grace, who as well as working on her team before moving to a community role, was one of Allie's closest friends.

'I only have a minute or two,' she said to him. Glancing around, she could see no one else. 'How come you got here so early?'

'A mate of mine lives off Park Avenue and messaged me,' he told her. 'Anything you can share?'

'Not yet. Too early for details. But it's a female, a teenager. Didn't get home from a night out, perhaps. It's so sad.'

'If there's anything I can do at a later date, let me know. If you have information to spread widely, I'm your man.'

'You're a smooth talker, more like, Cole. You only want me when there's a story.'

Simon feigned hurt.

Allie shooed him away. 'Go on, be off with you.' She walked off, shouting over her shoulder, 'I'll let you know as soon as, yeah?'

'You'd better!'

She smirked. Thank God for Simon. If she had to work, or rely on, people like Will Lawrence, the smarmy reporter from *Staffordshire News*, she wouldn't want to share a thing. And news and their reporters made things easier for the police at times. They weren't all as creepy as Lawrence who never minded spilling things he shouldn't.

Rejoining her team to find Jenny gone, Allie sought out Perry, and they made their way to her car. It was time to upset another family with the devastating news.

CHAPTER SEVEN

Seven months ago

Katie Frost had known Ethan Riley long before they finally got talking. To say she thought Ethan was out of her league was an understatement. She and her friend, Beth, had seen him and his brother, Isaac, around for a while at different places. A small city like Stoke-on-Trent meant they bumped into the same people all the time.

The city was split into six towns, and yet people rarely wandered far from where they lived. She and Beth would see the brothers mostly hanging around the boxing club near to their homes.

Katie was with Beth in Flynn's nightclub when she next saw him. They went there most weekends. Her mum was always telling her that it used to be a great night out in Hanley, but now Flynn's was one of the only places open for a good time.

She bumped into Ethan coming out of the loo, of all

places. It was nearly one a.m. She wasn't a big drinker, yet she was pleasantly merry, hot and sticky from all the dancing. Luckily for her, she'd touched up her makeup.

'It's Katie, right?' he asked, the music quieter out there in the corridor.

She nodded. 'It is.'

'I'm Ethan.'

'I know.'

They smiled at each other, moving to the side to let people pass.

'Are you on your own this evening?' he wanted to know.

'I'm with my friend, Beth, and a few other girls.'

'So no man in tow?'

Katie shook her head.

'Then let me buy you a drink.'

'Okay.'

Ethan took her hand, and they slalomed through the revellers, the music loud as they went back into the main room. He kept hold of it while he ordered her Bacardi and Coke and got himself a bottle of Becks. Katie saw Beth on the dance floor looking for her, so she waved to get her attention. When she spotted who Katie was with, Beth stuck two thumbs up.

They moved to a quieter area and sat down. Over the course of an hour or so, and another drink, they got to know each other. Ethan had a really nice smile close up, and piercing blue eyes. It sounded all Mills and Boon, but her heart really did flutter when he gazed at her, and when he kissed her for the first time, Katie was totally won over.

Beth sidled over to them eventually, waving apologetically. 'We're off now,' she said. 'Are you coming with us or...?'

'I can share a taxi home with you, if you like?' Ethan offered.

Katie glanced at Beth and then nodded at Ethan.

'Yes, thanks. Let's do that.'

With Beth appeased, Katie settled down with Ethan again. They left fifteen minutes later, and he was true to his word. She was home and in bed within half an hour. They'd arranged to meet tomorrow evening. Katie couldn't wait.

Of course, everyone knew Ethan had a reputation of being a bad boy. It was what drew Katie to him. All the boys she'd dated so far hadn't had rich parents either. Only one owned their own car, and that was a banger which kept breaking down. Ethan said he'd got a BMW for his eighteenth birthday last year. Katie knew she'd probably get a hundred quid for hers. Still, her mum tried her best. It was hard without Dad around now.

CHAPTER EIGHT

Allie drove to Ethan Riley's address, her mind buzzing about the events unfolding. Images of Katie Frost's body kept coming to her. Until the forensic team had turned up, Perry had quickly used crime scene tape to cordon off as much as possible to stop the public trampling over the field and pathway.

Now Allie was alert to the fact they were about to speak to one of the last people who'd seen Katie alive. For all they knew, Ethan might be the killer, but they would always keep an open mind. It was hard sometimes to stay impartial, but over the years they'd all learned to do it better with each murder case they'd been a part of.

It had taken fifteen minutes to get there, cutting through Hanley and along Leek New Road. Luckily the stormy clouds had abated, and the sun was blasting whenever it could through an intermittent cloudy sky.

She drove for a further couple of minutes and then took a left. There were six properties in the exclusive cul-de-sac. Allie spotted the one they were after by its name and pulled up outside. It was half past nine. Thankfully the curtains were open on all the windows she could see, and there were three cars on the drive in front of a double garage.

'Nice gaff.' Perry whistled. 'Must have cost a fortune.'

'I'll say. It's a five-bedroomed sprawl that was erected about thirty years ago. I know this because when Mark and I had been looking for our first home, we saw one similar for sale. I joked with him that we should think big and buy it. Back then it had a price tag of four hundred thousand, way out of our price range, for ever I expect, so goodness knows how much it's worth nowadays.' She rifled in the glove compartment until her hand fell on a tube of mints. 'Want one? I'd hate to go in smelling like a brewery.'

'You don't!'

'Even so. I was supposed to be going shopping with Poppy today, Manchester.'

'Watching the footie with Alfie, me.' Perry took one and popped it in his mouth. 'I was really looking forward to it.'

'Me, too. Still, at least our kids are safe.'

'Yep. Do you worry about the world they're growing up in nowadays?'

'Of course, but other than wrap them in blankets and not allow them out under any circumstances, how do we police that?'

Perry sniggered at her choice of words.

'And it is *so* nice to have someone to worry about,' she went on. 'I never thought I'd have to think of more than me and Mark.'

'Fostering suits you, Allie. You'll always be the mum of the team.'

'I don't know whether to treat that as a compliment or an insult,' she cried.

'Treat it in the manner it was given.'

Allie smiled. Then she opened the car door. 'Let's go do our stuff.'

With heavy footsteps, they approached the front door. The death knock was always an emotional roller coaster, even when it wasn't immediate family.

The door was opened by a woman in her forties. She was dressed in casual clothes, blonde hair scraped into a messy bun on the top of her head. She smiled at them politely. It was early Saturday morning; Allie assumed she'd be wondering what they wanted.

'Morning, it's Mrs Riley, isn't it?' Allie held up her warrant card, Perry following suit.

The woman's smile dropped, but she nodded.

'Is your son, Ethan, home?'

'Yes. Is everything okay?'

'May we come in, please?'

Mrs Riley moved to one side. They stepped into a large hallway, a stairway and several doors leading off it.

'The lounge is the first door on the right,' she told them. 'I'm Ruth. I'll shout Ethan down.'

'Thanks.'

They found themselves in an even larger room, a bay window at the front, bi-folding doors at the back. Three cream leather settees sat around an inglenook fire. Shocks of orange and caramel complemented the cushions and curtains. A mug of coffee and a plate were on a side table.

Allie noticed family photos and school portraits of two boys, who had a couple of years between them. It looked homely, the TV playing background tunes from a radio station on low.

Ruth popped her head around the door. 'Ethan will be down in a few minutes,' she said. Noticing the items on the table, she quickly scooped them up. 'Would you like a coffee, or tea?'

'A cup of tea would be great, thanks.' Allie wasn't going to look a gift horse in the mouth. She was parched, and a drink would warm her up too. 'We're sorry to interrupt your breakfast.'

'Oh, no. I've been up for ages. That was my second wind. Please, sit.'

Before she could leave the room again, a young man appeared in the doorway. Ethan was tall, broad, his black hair tousled. He was wearing a hastily pulled-on T-shirt, and jeans, and nothing on his feet.

'What's going on?' His eyes flitted from Allie to Perry to his mum.

'Come and take a seat,' Allie told him. 'We have some bad news.'

CHAPTER NINE

Ethan sat down on the settee, Ruth next to him.

'Is there anyone else at home?' Allie asked before she began.

'Only us at the moment,' Ruth informed them. 'My husband has gone into work first thing, with Isaac, my eldest son.'

Allie nodded. 'I'm sorry to inform you that a young woman was murdered last night, and we believe it to be Katie Frost.'

The two of them looked at her in disbelief. The news took a few seconds to filter into their brains before horror replaced it.

'No, that's wrong.' Ethan shook his head vehemently. 'I was with her last night. She was fine when I dropped her off.'

'Are you sure it's her?' Ruth asked, wiping away tears that fell freely.

'We haven't had a formal identification yet, but her family have been informed,' Allie replied. 'She had photo ID on a membership card which was found nearby. It had her address on it.'

Ethan gave out an animalistic roar and then stood up. 'No. It can't be her.' He removed his phone from his pocket.

Perry moved forward to stop him scrolling through it. As the screen went into awake mode, he saw unread message alerts flashing up.

He placed a hand on the boy's arm.

'Please, sit down again, Ethan,' Allie said. 'We have questions for you, and then I'm sure you have some for us. Mrs Riley, I'd love the tea now, if you don't mind?'

With his mother gone, Allie settled into her best friend mode to win the teenager's trust. It was imperative they got as much information from Ethan as possible as they took down the first account. He could also be a witness if he remembered anything significant.

'We had a row,' Ethan said, his head in his hands. 'We argued, and I drove off in a huff. Where was she killed?'

'We believe she was first attacked at the back of her home and then moved out of sight to the field behind.'

'Fuck.' Ethan gagged. 'It's all my fault. I should never have let her get out. I should have taken her to the door.'

'What time did you leave her?' Allie went on.

'About half eleven. We'd been to a party.'

'Can you tell me about that?'

'It was Abigail Matthews, her eighteenth. I picked Katie up, so I wasn't drinking. We were having a laugh, and then Katie started talking to one of her friends. I got mad, and we had a row. She wanted to go, and I didn't, but I'd brought her there, so we left. We were arguing for most of the drive back. She told me to stop the car and she would walk the rest of the way. She was so pissed with me. I figured I'd got the wrong end of the stick, but she wouldn't let me say sorry. In the end, she stormed off, slamming the door, and I screeched away like a prick.'

'Language, Ethan.' Ruth came into the room with a tray of drinks.

'Where was the party at?' Allie continued, wanting to confirm they were talking about the same one as Nate Frost had mentioned.

'The Bennett Cricket Club.'

'And the lad you said she was talking to?'

'She wasn't. I got a bit jealous, that's all. It was nothing.'

'All the same, I'd like to talk to him.'

'I don't know his name. But Abigail will. She lives in Smallthorne, on High Lane. Katie knows her, so her number will probably be stored in her phone.'

When they didn't comment, Ethan jumped to conclusions.

'You haven't got her phone?'

'The area is still being searched at the moment.' Allie wouldn't be drawn further.

Perry made a note of the details Ethan had given while she continued her questioning. 'And you say you left Katie about half past eleven? When would you have got home?'

'About quarter to twelve.'

'Were you up then, Mrs Riley?'

'No, Phil and I, that's my husband, were in bed about ten. He starts early on Saturdays and finishes at lunchtime. I was reading a book and switched off the lights at half past ten. I woke up at half past midnight when Isaac must have come in, but I went back to sleep.'

Allie was about to question her further but stopped. Mrs Riley hadn't heard anyone come in around quarter to midnight, but according to her, one of her sons came in around half past twelve. Because there were a number of possibilities in that alone.

Ethan might have come in, gone out again, and then come back in – indeed, they both might have done that.

Isaac could also have come in first and Ethan second and vice versa.

The fact she had seen neither of them would prove hard for either to have an alibi, too.

'Is there anything else you can tell us?' Allie asked next. 'Any reason why someone would want to do this to Katie?'

Ethan shook his head again. 'How did she...?'

'We're not releasing those details yet.'

'I need to see Donna.' Ethan stood up. 'Mum, will you take me?'

'Of course.'

'You may want to ring first,' Allie said.

Ethan nodded. 'I will, but I have to go. I have to say I'm sorry. If we hadn't rowed, she would still be alive.'

Allie and Perry looked at the carpet as the lad broke down, comforted by his mother. They had both seen all this before, acting to cover tracks. For now, they had no reason to assume Ethan was involved. His grief seemed sincere, but it could easily be guilt.

The evidence would tell them one way or the other. It always did.

CHAPTER TEN

Once the police had left, Ruth stared at the place where the car had been. Shock gripped her – poor Katie was dead? She'd only seen her two days ago. This couldn't be happening.

She came to her senses and rushed in to Ethan. He had his phone in his hands and was staring at the screen in disbelief. She sat down next to him. Seeing her child trying to keep his emotions in hurt her as much as she imagined he was in pain.

'Oh, love,' she said. 'I don't know what to say. I'm so sorry.'

Ethan sniffed, wiping a tear from his cheek. 'I don't think it will sink in for a while. I mean, who would do that to her?'

He broke then, and she pulled him into her arms.

'Did you see anyone hanging around as you dropped her off?'

'I – we had a row. She got out of the car a couple of streets back and walked home.'

'You *left* her on her own, in the middle of the night?' Ruth couldn't help herself. 'Why didn't you take her to her door?

She was your responsibility until then and...' She stopped, realising what she'd said.

Ethan glared at her. 'It's not my fault there's a maniac out there who would hurt her. How would I know that?'

'I didn't mean anything, son. I was talking in shock.' Ruth shook her head. 'I can't believe it.'

Ethan said nothing.

'Let me know when you want to go and see Katie's family. Perhaps we should leave them to grieve a little and go after lunch?' She patted his knee and stood up. 'We can call for flowers on the way. I'll take you, you're in no fit state to drive.'

Ethan nodded and shortly afterwards left the room.

While he was upstairs, Ruth called her husband.

'What's up? I'm in the middle of—'

'Oh, Phil. We've had some terrible news. The police have been. Katie was found dead last night. They came to tell Ethan.'

'What? How, when?' A pause. 'The police have been to our house?'

'Yes, she was attacked after he dropped her off last night. They won't say much yet.'

There was another pause. 'You don't think Ethan is involved in some way?'

'No!' She gave out a sob. 'But he was one of the last people to see her. She was supposed to be staying here. They had a row, so he took her home. I'm going to take him over there soon. He's distraught, Phil.'

'Christ. Have the police got any idea what happened?'

Ruth told him everything she knew.

'Ah, man. She was a nice girl.'

Ruth agreed. She'd had doubts about Katie when they first met. Ethan had been thrilled to bring her home and introduce them, and Ruth had been kind to Katie, but there had been something about her. She'd seemed shifty.

However, for the six months they'd been together now, her doubts had diminished, and she'd put it down to nerves. She'd enjoyed Katie's company. It was nice to have another female around the house, too, someone to moan with when the men were getting on her nerves. With three of them, she was often fetching and carrying and tidying up constantly.

But she was always here for them. And today was one of those times where she knew she'd be needed more than others.

'Do you want me to come home?' Phil said. 'I can get someone else to finish what I started.'

'No, you stay there. I'm taking Ethan over to Katie's, so there'll be nothing for you to do.'

Upstairs, Ethan paced his room as he heard his mum talking to his dad. Tears welled in his eyes again. He balled his hand into a fist and held it against his mouth for fear of shouting out. Katie couldn't be dead. He'd only seen her a few hours ago – imagine how it was going to look.

Everyone would blame him.

As his emotions got the better of him, so too did his temper. Whoever had killed Katie was going to get the wrath of him. When he found out what had happened, he would make sure someone paid.

Once he was calmer, he wiped his eyes and called Nate. His phone went to voicemail, so he disconnected the call. He'd be seeing him soon, so he sent a quick message to say he was sorry and that he was coming over.

Donna was going to be distraught. Ethan had always got on well with Katie's mum. She had a great sense of humour and treated him like family. Often, he felt more at home in her little house than he did in his own, without his brother breathing down his neck all the time.

He hoped Isaac had nothing to do with this. He'd caught him staring at Katie every now and then, had words about him leering. But Isaac had denied everything, said he didn't fancy Katie regardless. Could that be a ruse?

He wouldn't hurt her, would he?

But there was worse to think about. Ethan had given Katie a teddy bear last month. He'd said it was a gift to say how much he thought of her, but it was more than that. Ethan had managed to copy some footage of a crime being committed onto a memory stick and hidden it inside the teddy's clothes, knowing it would be safer at Katie's house than his own. With a brother like Isaac, he always needed a backup plan. A security net, whatever you wanted to call it.

And yet now, he would have to get the stick back, before the police got wind of it.

Because, as well as getting Isaac into a lot of trouble, Ethan would be toast if his brother found out he had something on him.

Brother or no brother, there was no love lost between them. Being the youngest, Ethan had lived in Isaac's shadow all his life. He'd never been able to do anything of his own accord without Isaac copying him or wanting in, so he could prove he was the better man.

When Ethan had joined Kennedy's Boxing Club, Isaac had taken no interest in the sport until then, and now, each time they sparred when he came along, he had to be the better man. Isaac thrived on taking people down.

Most of the time Ethan got on with his brother, and it was great to have him by his side. Others he was a pain, unpredictable, a show-off, a force he couldn't control.

It was why they were both involved in things their parents knew nothing about. Ethan hoped they'd never find out but, for now, it was worth the risk.

Unless Katie's murder brought the police sniffing around things they shouldn't know about.

CHAPTER ELEVEN

There was no answer at the first two houses Frankie tried in Park Avenue. Pushing a contact card through the letterbox of the second one, he moved to a third and knocked. He thought there might not be anyone home there, too, until he heard a kerfuffle behind the door.

'Just a minute!' a woman's voice shouted.

Frankie listened to the chain being pulled across before the door opened a couple of inches. A woman who seemed to be in her mid-sixties popped her head around the door.

'Morning, I'm sorry to bother you so early.' Frankie showed his warrant card and introduced himself. 'There's been an incident on the fields behind your property, so we're talking to everyone in the vicinity to see if they have any information.'

She scrutinised his ID badge. 'I'm not sure I can tell you much,' she said, 'but do come on in.'

The dog at her feet yapped as he stepped inside the hallway.

'Be quiet, Lottie.' The woman shooed her into the kitchen.

Before he got on to what had happened, over small talk, Frankie found out her name was Liz Mason, and she'd lived in the house for the past forty-one years. Liz had been a widow for four years, knew a lot of the neighbours, but mostly kept herself to herself. She'd raised her daughter there, and now her grandson, Tommy, who was eighteen. He'd stayed when his mum had moved to Scotland. Liz enjoyed his company. After that information overload, Frankie very much assumed he'd found the top gossiper around there.

'The street hasn't changed much, to be fair,' Liz went on. 'You hear about places getting rougher as younger people move in, but that hasn't happened here. Of course, not everyone behaves themselves all the time.'

Frankie sensed more scandal coming his way and leaned in closer. 'Oh?'

Liz stopped then. 'I don't mean anyone in particular,' she insisted. 'So what's happened? I haven't heard the news on the radio yet, but I know something is going on.'

Moving to sit at the kitchen table, Frankie waited until she'd joined him.

'I'm sorry to tell you that a young woman has been killed. We believe it to be one of your neighbours but for now we're not revealing any names.'

'Oh no.' Liz's hand shot to her chest. 'Is it going to be someone I know?'

'More than likely, I'm sorry. I was wondering if you saw or heard anything out of the ordinary last night between the hours of eleven p.m. and one a.m.'

Liz sat forward.

'As a matter of fact, something did happen to us last night. That's me and Lottie.' She stroked the dog affectionately and let her up on her knee. 'I take her out every night around half past eleven. We only go along the path and back. Lottie is getting on now, so can't walk far, bless. We were nearly at the gate to come back in when I heard pounding footsteps. Lottie barked, startling a man, and he almost walked right into me.'

Frankie sat forward at this news and took out his notepad.

'He swore and then told me to watch where I was going. I was about to reply but he pushed past and ran.'

'And what time would that be?'

'Oh, I don't know for sure, but we're usually out around fifteen minutes.'

'Did you see what the man looked like?'

'Not really. He wore a hoodie, pulled over his head, and the collar of his jacket turned up. I couldn't even tell you what colour his hair or eyes were. It was so dark. There're only a couple of lights either end of the run. I'm sorry.'

'Don't be. This could be significant information. Often when we get further into an investigation, evidence no matter how small suddenly fits together.'

A silence dropped on the room.

'Where was Tommy last night?'

'He went to some party, at the cricket club.'

'Do you know what time he got home?'

'No, I was in bed and asleep. But it would have been after midnight as that was the last time I looked at the clock before switching off the bedside lamp.' She stroked the head of the little dog. 'What a dreadful business. I hope it isn't anyone I know. You don't feel safe in your own property these days.'

'There'll be a huge police presence over the next week or so. I hope that will ease your mind.'

'Well, I pray you catch whoever it was, the sooner the better.'

Frankie left shortly afterwards, disappointed but hopeful

nonetheless. Insignificant details often turned out to be case breakers. He hoped whoever the man was would come forward once Liz Mason's information was given out to the public. At the very least, it might rule someone out of their enquiries.

Or rule them in as a person of interest.

CHAPTER TWELVE

Donna rinsed the cups in the sink, staring out of the window at nothing in particular. Thank goodness she wasn't able to see the field from where she was. All she had in front of her now was the brick wall separating her from her neighbour.

She felt like she was trapped, seeing that wall. No way forward, no way back. In a matter of seconds, her life had changed. Katie was dead, she was never coming home. Her family were disintegrating around her. How was she going to live without her?

Katie had been the baby of the family and, even at seventeen, she would wrap them all around her little finger. She was a stubborn miss, determined, feisty. But she was kind, funny, and so loving. She was always after a hug, never afraid to show her emotions. She'd come into the kitchen each morning in her pyjamas and throw her arms around Donna's neck, ask how she was.

After the initial shock of the police turning up with the news, Donna's tears had dried. She had to be strong for Shona and Nate and save her grief for when she was alone. She would be the one people would want to talk to, express their disbelief and sympathies as news filtered through. She was dreading it.

Despite that, while they were on their own, she needed to talk to Shona and Nate. She made fresh drinks, even though she didn't want another, and sat down with them. Jacob was sitting next to Shona now, so she took the seat by Nate.

Jacob was tall with short blond hair, and a cheeky boy smile that would have forgiven him quite a lot of things if it wasn't for a set of crooked teeth. His dad had knocked one of his lower ones out when he was younger, and he'd never had it replaced. But he was a respectable lad, providing for her daughter, and that was all that mattered to Donna.

She looked at them each in turn. Shona was leaning her head on Jacob's shoulder, eyes raw from crying. Jacob comforted her, rubbing at her arm while he stared at the table. Nate was close to tears but trying not to show how upset he was.

Donna was prepared to turn her head for her children as long as they were safe. Because she knew something had been going on.

'This might be the only time we get to ourselves as a family for a while,' she said. 'So I want to ask you some questions. I have to find out who would do this, and why. Is there anything you know about Katie that she wanted to keep from me? It doesn't matter if it's something bad. I have to know.'

Shona lifted her head and then shook it. 'She was happy, Mum. Reminded me of you and Dad.'

Donna swallowed. Bringing up Max's name brought a bolt of grief she hadn't felt in a while rushing back to her. How she wished he was here now, to help her get through this. He'd know what to do, too, to find out the truth.

'Ethan wouldn't hurt her, Mum,' Nate joined in. 'If that's what you're thinking.'

'I'm not. I'm trying to make sense of what's happened. Was she okay at college? No one was causing trouble for her?'

'She never said, if so, and I'm sure she'd tell me that.' Shona wiped at her eyes as more tears fell. 'I don't understand it at all.'

'She would always watch out for her family,' Jacob spoke. 'She was protective around Shona and the baby, and she wanted Nate to do well. And she wanted you, Donna, to be happy again.'

'She told you all that?' Donna was surprised.

'Yeah, I gave her a lift to college the other morning. She was really chatty.'

Donna sat back in the chair, feeling claustrophobic all of a sudden. She recalled how she'd felt the same when Max died. He'd been in a hospice for his final days, and they'd been able to visit around the clock. One of them had practically spent every waking minute with him until he'd gone.

But this was different. At least they'd been able to say farewell to Max. Katie had been out there alone, perhaps for the night, a few metres away, and yet no one had been with her because they hadn't known.

She held in a sob, hoping not to upset anyone further. But it was hard.

They'd have to move. How could she look out of the bedroom window now, onto the field where her daughter had been slain? Yes, slain. It was a strong word, but it was true. Memories like those wouldn't heal over the years.

Every time she went out or came home, she would see where it had happened, think about what had gone on and why. People around them would know, eye them with sympathy. She couldn't bear it. At least she was the only one who came in the back way. The kids mostly used the front door, due to being dropped off or picked up in cars on the street.

Yet Donna knew she couldn't leave the area, nor the

house. She would be connected to this place for the rest of her life, close to her youngest.

'Is there anything else you *need* to tell me?' she asked next as everyone sat in silence.

Fleeting glances between the three of them said there was. She wondered if it was anything to do with Katie, or were there other secrets they had?

Donna waited for one of them to speak, but when nothing was forthcoming, she sighed in exasperation. Whatever it was would have to wait.

CHAPTER THIRTEEN

The doorbell went, and Donna got to her feet again, wondering who the first person to call would be. They'd have to start telling people soon. Donna had lost her own parents during her twenties, and Max's dad had been dead for over a decade. There was just his mum, Val. She was going to be devastated. Katie was the baby of the family in her eyes.

A woman stood on the pavement, next to a man in police uniform. He was facing out to the street.

'Mrs Frost?' she said. 'I'm PC Rachel Joy and I'm a Family Liaison Officer. I'm so very sorry for your loss. May I come in, please?'

Donna showed her through to the living room. 'The man outside?'

'He'll be keeping a record of who comes in and goes out of the property.' Rachel raised a hand when Donna went to speak. 'It's standard procedure. We want to ensure you don't have unwanted visitors today. Anyone can come and go, that's not a problem, but you might become overwhelmed with all the messages of condolence.'

Donna could only nod in reply, her body seeming not to

belong to her anymore. Seeing this woman, another police officer, made it even more real that Katie was dead. She'd wanted to keep it together for her family, but tears poured from her eyes, and she began to shake.

Even resolving not to break down, Donna cracked. Her legs turned to jelly, and Rachel put a hand out to steady her before she fell to the floor.

'Sit down for a moment.' Rachel guided her to the settee.

Donna cried for the family, for Ethan, for anyone who knew her beautiful daughter. But, most of all, she cried for the sweet teenager who would never walk through that front door again.

As soon as Donna was out of hearing range, Nate ran a hand through his hair. 'I can't believe Katie is dead. It doesn't seem real.'

'Look.' Jacob gnawed at his bottom lip. 'I hate to bring this up now, but we need to talk about what was said to the police, and what we say from now on. We don't want any of us tripping up about last night.'

'Is that all you're interested in, keeping your nose clean?' Nate glared at Jacob. 'Our sister is dead.'

'And we could be in big trouble if anyone finds out what we were doing.' Jacob glanced at them both.

'No one will find out.'

'Have you two been up to something else?' Shona eyed them with suspicion. 'Because you weren't at home when you said you were, and if I'm covering up because of some cock-up that will bring trouble to my door, then you'd better tell me.'

'Be quiet!' Jacob lowered his voice. 'We were only doing the usual. There's no need to broadcast it.'

'And are you clean, if the police search the house?'

'Yes, I'm clean!' Nate scraped his chair back and walked towards the door. 'I can't do this. I'm going to get some air.'

'Don't go out the back way.' Shona reached for his arm as he went past. 'You remember what the detective said. You don't want to see anything—'

'I don't care. I just need to get out of here.'

'I'll come with you,' Jacob said.

'No, leave me alone.'

Nate slammed the door on his way out. If he didn't get away from the house, he was going to explode. His sister had been murdered, and all Jacob was concerned about was not getting caught for what they'd been up to the night before. Nate didn't care about that right now. All he wanted to know was who had done that to Katie.

He opened the gate onto the pathway. He could see a group of police at the far end, and a white tent. He wondered what was happening in there.

He stood watching what was going on across the fields. There was a tent there, too, crime scene tape across the path holding people back.

'Fucking vultures,' he muttered. Then he spotted Liz Mason popping her head out for a nosy and retreated back inside. He couldn't face anyone.

Not today.

CHAPTER FOURTEEN

Six months ago

Katie got to know Ethan a lot over the next few weeks. She found his bad-boy image a bit hit and miss. When they were with other people, he'd often be aloof with her, and could be seen as possessive. When they were alone, he'd be much better. A softer side came out, but he could be quite nasty if she pushed his buttons.

She recalled one occasion when she'd said hello to an ex she'd dated last year, and Ethan was asking all sorts of questions about him. He got all moody when she said she was with him for six months. She couldn't understand why as he was with another girl before they'd started dating. *He'd* moved on.

Ethan was much better than his brother, though. Isaac was two years older than Ethan, and he wanted to be in charge all the time, the bossy one. Katie didn't like him much. There was something about him she couldn't quite put her finger on. He'd say snide remarks that only she would hear, but she tried not to let them bother her. He was jealous of Ethan, she thought.

They both worked in the family business, which was mainly property development. In his spare time, Ethan was mostly at the boxing club. Often when they went out, Ethan had to pick something up, or drop a package off, on their way to wherever they were going. He didn't like her to go in with him, so she'd sit in the car. But he made it worth her while when she was with him.

It was exciting and nerve-racking when he invited her to meet his parents. It took her ages to figure out what to wear. And as she was leaving the house, her mum collared her.

'Off somewhere nice with Ethan?' she asked.

Katie nodded. 'We're going for something to eat.'

'You look gorgeous, love. He's brought a twinkle to your eye. When am I going to meet him?'

'Soon,' she fibbed. She wasn't about to say she wanted to see how that evening went first because she was ashamed to bring him home. 'Don't wait up!' she shouted over her shoulder and then swept out before she could say anything else.

Ethan's house was amazing. Katie had visited several times when there'd been no one at home. Beth had been so jealous when she'd told her he had his own bathroom. And no piddly en suite. He had a proper bathroom, with a bath and a separate shower unit. The first time they'd got together, they went up to his room and shared a shower. It was so much fun, although she was terrified at being caught with him. Luckily, no one came home unexpected.

Ethan wasn't the first man she'd slept with, but he was a lot more experienced than her. He wasn't rough like she'd thought he'd be because of his image. But he did like to be dominant, so she let him mostly. Katie could tell he worked out a lot. She loved running a hand over his pecs.

When they arrived at his house that evening, Ethan showed her into the living room, his hand firmly wrapped around hers. His mum and dad were sitting on the settee. Isaac wasn't there, thankfully.

His mum smiled at her and welcomed her into her arms.

Katie saw a real beauty. She wasn't one of those women who made themselves worse as they'd aged by having fake this and that. Everything about her seemed natural, although Katie obviously couldn't tell if she dyed her hair. It was brunette, wavy to her shoulders with a side fringe. Her eyes were made up expertly and her clothes were wowzers. She seemed as if she'd stepped out of a catalogue for women in their forties who looked ten years younger. Katie warmed to her straightaway.

'I'm Ruth. It's lovely to meet you at last,' Ruth told her. 'Ethan never stops talking about you. You've certainly captured his heart.'

'Mum,' Ethan cried, a hint of red showing on his cheeks.

'I'm Phil,' Ethan's dad said, getting up to shake her hand. He kissed her lightly on the cheek and smiled. He was very much like Ethan and Isaac, with short black hair, deep blue eyes, and a shapely physique, although with a slight paunch, and he was smart in dark jeans and a white shirt.

'Nice to meet you both,' Katie found her voice at last, a little overwhelmed. But if it was noticeable, neither of them commented.

'Let's eat.' Ruth clapped her hands and pointed to a table set out in the orangery at the back of the room. 'I did check with Ethan what your tastes were, so I hope you like chilli con carne.'

'Fine by me, thanks for the invite, Mrs Riley.'

'Ruth, please. Mrs Riley makes me feel so old.'

They scooted across to the table, and Ethan squeezed Katie's hand. She gave him a grateful smile before they sat down. She was so nervous she knew her mouth would run away with her, and she'd end up embarrassing herself by saying something stupid. But Mrs Riley – Ruth – seemed to have gone to a lot of trouble so she'd have to try her best to be sensible.

Because she wanted to be a part of this family so much.

CHAPTER FIFTEEN

Frankie was sitting in the front room of number twenty-two Park Avenue, having been called in once uniform had seen the residents. He wanted to clarify the statement a little so had popped along to get more details.

The people who lived there were Edna and her sister, Florence. They were both in their early eighties and could pass as twins as, by the look of things, there didn't seem to be too many years between them.

Edna was smaller than Florence, her back arched, and she walked with a stick. Both women had thin lips and eyes hidden within wrinkles, their round faces framed by grey curls.

Florence wore a checked dress and black tights with bootee slippers. She reminded Frankie of his great-grandmother in some ways, and it made him smile. He warmed to her instantly once she'd offered a cup of tea which accompanied a huge plate of biscuits.

'Can you tell us anything else about what has happened?' Florence said, taking control of the tea pouring.

Frankie watched Florence's hands shaking as she passed a cup to him, seeing he would have more tea in the saucer.

'We can't say much more at the moment, I'm afraid.' He knew they were after information as they would have been told what they could before he'd arrived. 'You mentioned to the officer who called earlier that you heard voices last night on the path. Can you tell me more about that?'

'We were off to bed, weren't we, Edna?' Florence said. 'We always stay up late as neither of us sleep well.'

'And what time was this?'

'Shortly after half past eleven. Isn't that right, Edna?'

'Yes, that's right,' Edna joined in.

Frankie smiled at her, hoping this wasn't going to take long. He took a mouthful of tea, trying not to grimace at its weakness. There was too much milk for his liking. One or two sips would be polite, he mused.

'My room is at the back of the house,' Florence continued, 'and I heard noises so shouted through to Edna. We opened the window quietly and listened.'

Frankie took notes of the conversation.

'We heard a man and a woman arguing.'

'Did you hear what they were saying?'

'We couldn't make much of it out, just the tone of their voices.'

'So there was one man and one woman. Were their accents local?'

'I think so.' Florence nodded.

Frankie knew this could be something or nothing. Unless anyone else had seen or heard a couple arguing, there wasn't enough detail to make use of.

Edna suddenly sat forward and shouted, 'Don't walk away from me.'

Frankie, who was about to take another mouthful of the tea, jumped, more liquid sloshing into the saucer.

'Edna!' Florence chastised. 'What on earth are you yelling for?'

'That's what he said. Don't walk away from me.'

'Oh, that's brilliant. Anything else?' Frankie encouraged now his heart rate was slowing again.

Edna sat for a moment in thought and then shook her head.

'The woman he was talking to didn't say anything in return?'

'I'm not sure but I heard him say that as plain as day.'

'And there were no screams or cries for help?' Frankie wanted to make sure he took everything down right.

'Nothing.' Florence shuddered. 'Then we went to bed.'

Frankie smiled politely. Another quick drink of the tea, and he placed it back on the tray. 'You've been a great help,' he said. 'I'll leave you to it.'

'There was an argument again after that, and then it went quiet, so we closed the window. We often hear people bickering on their way home, don't we, Edna? We're not far from the pub.'

It was time to leave. Frankie thanked them for the tea and left contact cards with his details on. 'Again, thank you for the information.'

Once outside, he glanced up and down to see officers talking to residents and groups of people on doorsteps or huddled together on the pavement chatting among themselves.

He couldn't help thinking how these kinds of events affected communities in the long run. Every one of these people had got up to enjoy a quiet Saturday morning, perhaps having plans scuppered because of the goings-on.

But he also knew that each one could be helpful to the police in a community like this one, too.

Unless that person was involved, of course.

CHAPTER SIXTEEN

Donna's head was pounding. It was only just gone eleven, and she didn't know how she was going to get through the rest of the day. Her friend, Hannah, had rung immediately after she'd sent her a message to say that something terrible had happened. She'd spoken to her over the phone then, and Hannah had asked if she could come around.

When there was a knock at the door, Rachel went to get it. Moments later, Hannah came bursting into the room. Her daughter, Beth, and husband, Wes, followed close behind. Donna had known Hannah since they were in their twenties. She had a motherly figure and short blonde hair, but it was the bark of her laughter that got her noticed most. The two of them had often fallen about in jest long after a joke because Hannah sounded like a seal when she couldn't stop.

There was no laughter today. Sombre faces from Beth who had her mum's hair colouring and her dad's lanky build. Wes had turned forty last month, and despite all their teasing of him getting old, he was doing so with grace. His hair was sporting a few streaks of grey, glasses with navy-blue frames bringing out the colour of his eyes.

'Oh, Donna, I'm so sorry,' Hannah cried, rushing to her.

Donna's tears started long before arms were wrapped around her. 'She's dead, Hannah, she's dead,' she sobbed. 'Who would do this to her?'

Hannah rubbed a soothing hand up and down Donna's back. 'Have the police said how it happened?'

Donna relayed what she could, while Rachel made more tea. It seemed awkward yet comforting having a police officer in the kitchen with them.

When the tea was made, they moved through to the living room and sat down. A shocked silence dropped.

'I can't believe she's gone.' Beth burst into tears. 'She was my best friend. What am I going to do without her?'

Hannah, who was sitting next to Donna, glanced at Wes, hoping he would go and comfort their daughter. Surprisingly, he did. Beth sobbed in his arms for a moment, while he wiped tears from his eyes.

'I would have brought Mitchell with me, but he's feeling ill.' Hannah scoffed. 'From the smell coming from his room, I'd say he'd been drinking a little too much at the party last night, but I'll leave that for later.'

'It's fine, Han.' Donna blew her nose. 'He doesn't have to come. I think we'll all deal with this in our own way.'

Rachel liked the simple task of tea making when she was in family liaison mode. It was a job well done as she often gleaned things when people either wanted to talk to her, or who she could chat with to gain more information.

She was making fresh drinks in the kitchen when Beth came in.

'Would you like a mug of tea while I'm making?' she asked.

'No, thanks, but my mum would, please.'

'How is your mum?' Rachel continued, trying not to show her back too much. 'I assume you're all close with your mums being friends?'

'Yes, we all grew up together. It was hard for Dad when Max died – that's Katie's dad. He said that their square which worked so well was now a triangle with a huge part missing. I thought it was a strange analogy, but I understand what he means now.'

'So you know Katie well?'

'Yes, she was my best friend.'

'Is there anything you can share with us, that might help us find who did this to her? I'm sure she would have told you things she wouldn't tell anyone else. It's not tittle-tattling when it could help with our investigations.'

Tears welled in the girl's eyes as she tried and failed to control her emotions.

Rachel passed her a tissue. 'Let me take these through and then we can have a chat.'

She was gone for a matter of minutes, thinking Beth wouldn't be there when she got back, but she found her sitting at the table. She had her hands wrapped around a mug.

'Hope you don't mind,' she said. 'I decided I would have a coffee.'

Rachel reached for the drink she'd made for herself and sat opposite her. 'Your mum is comforting Mrs Frost. I'm glad she has someone close to her. Had you known Katie long?'

'Since junior school. We'd been best friends all that time.'

'It must be so hard to comprehend at the moment. What was Katie like?'

Beth smiled, her eyes watering again. 'She was kind, funny, and we made each other laugh. I could say anything to her, and she wouldn't tell a soul.' She grimaced. 'Not that I have any secrets about her. We did everything together. College, shopping, nights out at the pub, although we can't drink yet.'

Rachel smiled to show she wasn't bothered about the minutiae. Most teenagers got into a pub before they were eighteen, drinking or not.

'Was there anyone she was worried about?'

CHAPTER SEVENTEEN

'There are a couple of things that come to mind.' Beth paused and looked to the door before she continued talking to Rachel. 'Me and Katie had a bit of mither where we worked. We did a few weekends working at the minimart on the high street, but we left because the owner's son was a lech. He got far too close to us for our liking.'

'Can you be more specific?' Rachel's hackles were raising at the thoughts running through her head.

'He was all talk really, but it wasn't nice banter to listen to. Everything he said to us, he used sexual innuendos, and when we didn't laugh along, he'd pretend he was joking, trying to get down with the kids. He's twenty-five. We ignored him mostly, but that's why we left.'

'And you say it's on the high street?'

'Yes, on the corner of Dartmoor Road. We don't go in at all now. We use the newsagents instead.' Beth swallowed as she talked about Katie in the present tense. 'I can't believe she's dead. What am I going to do without her?'

Rachel made a mental note to get someone to the minimart to check out this man, see what he had to say about his behaviour. It wasn't right that young women were exploited that way. Beth was a beautiful woman, Katie, too. Rachel could imagine how many heads they turned when they were together.

'You mentioned there were a couple of things?' she said then.

Beth paused, looking sheepish. 'Katie changed since she and Ethan started dating. We fell out two weeks ago.'

'About what?'

'I'm not sure Ethan is into her as much as he says. I saw him talking to another girl, and he seemed way too friendly. But when I told Katie, she accused me of being jealous because she'd landed him, and I was on my own. It wasn't anything like that. I wanted to make sure she was okay. I-I thought he was using her.'

'Why would you think that?'

Beth shrugged. 'I don't know, but pretty soon, he was seeing her every night, and she started to buy herself things. I saw her with a wad of money once. She said Ethan had given it to her as he was taking her shopping.'

'Was it her birthday?'

'No.'

'Perhaps he was treating her.' Rachel smiled, refraining from getting her notepad in case Beth clammed up. She was eager to know more so she stayed quiet.

Beth was about to continue when the door opened and Nate came in. He was trying to keep his face neutral, but Rachel could see how affected he was by his sister's death.

'Want a coffee?' she asked.

Nate shook his head. Rachel decided it was time to go back to the living room to join the others. Her job was one of discretion, so she had to learn as much as she could. But there were a few interesting titbits there that she could pass on to the Major Crimes Team.

. . .

'What did you say to her? You know she's police?' Nate turned to Beth.

'She was asking about our friendship.'

'So do you know anything about why she died?'

'Of course not!' Beth shook her head vehemently. 'You know we fell out. I hadn't seen or heard from her, in like, two weeks. I hated that. But she chose Ethan over me. It was bound to happen one day. We can't be two peas in a pod all our lives.'

Nate paused and turned to stare out of the window. 'Did he treat her well?'

Beth was torn. If she said too much, she might get the wrath of one of the Riley brothers. But Katie was Nate's sister, and he had a right to know if she'd been in trouble. In the end, she said a little about both.

'I told her to be careful around Ethan, and she didn't like it. She said I was jealous, but I was watching out for her, that's all. She seemed smitten with Ethan, so he must have been kind to her.'

'What about Isaac?'

Beth lowered her eyes. 'I don't know anything about him.'

'So she didn't tell you about the shower incident?'

Beth looked up sharply. 'I said I wouldn't tell anyone.'

CHAPTER EIGHTEEN

It was nearing midday when Allie arrived at the police station with Perry. She'd sent Frankie a message to come in for a briefing. She wanted to know what was being said on Park Avenue, plus she was sure Sam would have been doing some stellar intel work.

And she needed food.

She and Perry nipped along to Piccadilly to grab a bite to eat for everyone. It would be a working lunch while they caught up. They joined the queue at the deli counter.

'Any thoughts on events so far, Perry?' Allie asked once they'd placed their order.

'Only how young she is to go so soon.' Perry kept his voice low so as not to alarm people nearby.

'I've been wondering if it will be a one-off or if it's something we should be thinking might happen again.'

'Hiya, you two,' the woman behind the counter said. 'Terrible news about that wee girl in Smallthorne. Any news of a name yet?'

'Nothing we can share, Mandy, I'm afraid,' Allie replied.

'I heard it was a horrible attack. Someone mentioned multiple stab wounds on Facebook?'

Allie and Perry glanced at each other surreptitiously. It wasn't even true. Everyone seemed to be an armchair detective nowadays.

'There will be details online shortly,' Allie said noncommittally. She gave the woman a faint smile.

Mandy handed over their sandwiches, and they made their way back to the station.

'Saturday overtime?' an officer on the front desk teased.

'Yeah, we like a murder to entertain us at the weekend,' Allie joked. 'It might be you next if you don't stop with the quips.'

He laughed loud and hearty as Allie and Perry shared a smile. They walked through the door on the left and up a flight of stairs to their office, the door opening to a noisy rabble sitting around the desks. Frankie was hovering above Sam's screen as she was showing him something.

'Anything interesting?' Allie asked, handing out the grub to the relevant people.

Murmurs of thanks went around the room.

'I was viewing some CCTV that had come in.' Sam pointed to it. 'There are several people walking around within half an hour either side of the time Frankie told me his witnesses saw or heard people, and half a dozen others who've rung to say they were in the vicinity.' She handed a piece of paper to Allie. 'I've made a list with contact details for any that we need to check over.'

'Thanks, we can follow up with these after lunch.'

Allie ate her sandwich standing up while she listened to their updates. 'Frankie, did you get anything useful?' she asked first.

'Yes and no.' Frankie told them about Edna and Florence FitzJohn, and then Liz Mason. 'Mrs Mason didn't give me much of a description of the suspect, but she did say from his voice and build that it was a man.'

'That's interesting,' Perry commented. 'I wonder if it was Ethan and Katie arguing.'

'Once we've worked out who went along the walkway and at what times, we may be able to eliminate any couples who could have been around, and if there aren't any at the time, it could mean it was them. That's a great start.' Allie turned to Sam. 'Can you check out who went in and out of the back way at that time, please?'

'It's not covered by CCTV, boss. Only from the main road. I am checking the vicinity, though.'

'Thanks. Perry, tell them about Ethan Riley while I finish my sarnie.'

Perry relayed the details of their conversation and gave Sam a piece of paper with a number plate written on it. 'Ethan has a black Audi.'

'Ah, I've seen that.' Sam looked again. 'It's parked up for about a minute and then leaves at eleven-twenty. He speeds off in a hurry.'

'Check to see if he comes up again or parks somewhere else,' Allie told her. 'And then filter that through to the timeline, please.' She paused. 'All plausible pieces of a puzzle, but it's how to fit them together to make it all work.' She wiped her hands on a paper napkin. 'It's a start, though. Sam, what have you picked up on the socials?'

'Lots of posts about Katie's murder in general. I've been making a list of as and when she is mentioned. With regards to Katie's page on Facebook, everything seems above board. I've scrolled through for a few months and there's nothing weird mentioned. Oodles of selfies with a guy who I know now is Ethan Riley. Many with friends, too. She seems to be really popular. I'll dig into the other channels soon. Oh, and there's a vigil taking place at six p.m. tomorrow evening. It's being arranged by one of her friends, Beth Lightwood. Everyone has been asked to wear pink, and lay flowers if they want to, light candles, that kind of thing.'

'We need to attend that, mingle in the crowd. Jenny will do a press release soon, and then we can start talking to Katie's closest friends once the body has been identified. What about the family itself, Sam?'

'Nothing coming up. No criminal records.'

'And Jacob Chetwyn? He's Katie's sister's fella.'

Sam typed his name into the PNC, and an image flashed up. 'Is this him?'

Allie nodded.

'He has several charges, mainly for petty theft.' Sam skimmed the details on the screen. 'No prison spells, though. A caution for cannabis.'

'May be worth keeping an eye on his movements. This is great work, Sam, thanks.' She looked at the team in general. 'Now all we need to do is get our heads down and see what else we find.'

CHAPTER NINETEEN

The next visitor to arrive surprised Donna. She'd expected Ethan to come and see them, but not with his mum. Ruth Riley had never been to her home before, despite Katie and Ethan being an item for near on seven months. Then again, Donna had never been invited to visit the Riley household. And she couldn't return the favour anyway. Who could blame her, really, when she hadn't much to offer?

Ruth came into the room holding a large box of flowers wrapped in cellophane.

'Mrs Frost, Donna.' Ruth rushed over to her. 'I'm Ruth, Ethan's mum. Dreadful that we have to meet this way. I'm so sorry for your loss.'

'These are beautiful.' Donna took the flowers. She sniffed at a petal, lingering on its scent, before passing them to Shona. 'Can you put these in the living room, please?'

Shona nodded.

'Nice place you have here,' Ruth said, running an eye around the room. 'It's very homely. Mine is always messy with having two boys and my husband. It's like tidying up after children all the time.'

'Mum,' Ethan chided.

'What? Oh, sorry, am I being tactless?' Ruth shook her head. 'Forgive me.'

'Honestly, it's fine.' Donna glanced at Ethan, his broken face upsetting her. She remembered when Katie had first mentioned him to her. "Mum,'" she'd said with a beaming smile. "I've met someone." And when Donna had met him, too, he'd turned out to be quite nice. Polite and thoughtful.

'Could I use your bathroom, please?' Ethan asked.

'Yes, of course. You know where it is,' Donna's cheeks burned. How embarrassing not to have a downstairs loo. Katie had told her about the Riley's home a million times, shown her lots of photos until she'd been green with envy. She only prayed Nate hadn't left an empty toilet roll like he was prone to doing.

Ethan dashed upstairs. When he reached the landing, he glanced behind. Everyone was still in the kitchen and living room. He tiptoed across the carpet, hoping not to find any loose floorboards that would alert anyone he was snooping around.

He pressed down the door handle. It was a long room, split in two to accommodate both Katie and Nate. He'd only been in a handful of times when no one had been home. Even without the smell of sweaty feet and sleep in this one, the navy-blue duvet and dark clothes hanging on a rail in the corner, he would know this part was Nate's.

With no time to lose, he stepped inside. This section was dressed in lemons and whites, block colours, stripes and squares. He sniffed, the aroma of Katie's signature perfume making his eyes water. Her name was on a light board by the side of her bed.

Spying the white teddy bear on the pillow, he reached for

it. He searched the pockets of the red dungarees it was wearing, but he couldn't find it.

It had to be in there somewhere. He pulled back the duvet, peered underneath the pillows, and then stooped to peek under the bed. Where was it?

'What are you doing?'

Ethan jumped to his feet and turned around, a hand on his chest but relaxing a little when he saw it was his mum.

'I was taking one last look in her room. I... I suppose I wanted to connect with her one more time.'

'Oh, love.' Ruth rushed over to offer her son comfort. 'I know this is going to be so hard for you to get through.'

He said nothing as she held on to him. He needed her to think he was upset, that he couldn't bear to be without Katie. It was true in a way, but he'd feel better when he'd found what he had come for.

'We need to go downstairs before we're found sneaking around,' Ruth said. 'Maybe you should ask Donna if you can have something from Katie's room, to remind you of her. I think she'd like that.'

'Yeah, I will, later.' Ethan was already planning on coming back again either way.

'Ethan?'

He was at the top of the stairs when he turned to face her.

'You know you can talk to me about anything, don't you? I'm here for you and I won't be quick to judge, no matter what.'

His eyes widened. 'You think I killed Katie?'

'No, that's not what I mean at all!'

'Well, I didn't but I'm going to find out who did.' His face thunderous, Ethan marched downstairs with his mum following behind. He was disappointed he hadn't got what he'd come for.

Because he had to find that memory stick before anyone else did.

Before the Lightwood family left, everyone gave Donna a hug. Afterwards, she went upstairs to escape for a few minutes. She hid away in the bathroom. It was the only place she could guarantee not being interrupted.

She stared at the mirror until her eyes blurred due to her tears. This was a nightmare, wasn't it? She was going to wake up soon, then laugh it off as the worst thing ever. And then Katie would come through the door, say she was starving and ask what was for tea, sling her bag on the table and her coat across the chair.

How she missed her little foibles already.

What was she going to do without her?

CHAPTER TWENTY

After finding out the address of the party girl from the Bennett Cricket Club, Frankie set off to speak to her. She lived local to the club on High Lane, and he was in awe when he pulled up outside a beautiful pre-war detached house.

Frankie loved anything traditional, not like the new-build semi he and Lyla were living in at the moment. They'd recently put their home up for sale with a view to moving to something similar, although with their budget, it would have to be another semi-detached.

There was always a downside to every property, though, he mused, as the noise of the traffic going past was deafening when he opened the car door.

'Mrs Matthews? I'm DC Higgins.' Frankie held up his warrant card. 'I was wondering if I could talk to you and your daughter, if she's home?'

'Yes, she's here, with her friend, Harriet. Have you come about Katie Frost?'

'About the body found? Yes.' Sometimes Frankie hated how news travelled fast via word of mouth, but when it was calls like this one and he didn't have to relay details of the crime, he was quite grateful.

'It was awful to hear about it,' she said after she'd ushered him in and closed the front door. 'Abigail found out from Facebook, and she told me. I can't believe it. She was with us last night.'

'At the cricket club? That's what I'd like to talk to you, and her, about.'

'Go through. She's in the conservatory.'

'Beautiful home you have here,' he couldn't help saying.

'Thanks. I'm Tricia, by the way.'

Frankie followed her into the kitchen with a range of shaker units in sage green and cream, large slate tiles on the floor, a bright-red fridge freezer, and a dining table and settee. Beyond that, the picture window showed a walled garden area, creating a private terrace that would be an oasis if it wasn't for the noise outside.

On the settee, two girls huddled together, wearing slouch gear and thick ribbed socks. Their eyes were red and puffy, and they were looking at an iPad.

'Girls, this is a detective. There's nothing to worry about. He'd like some details about the party last night.' Tricia turned to Frankie and pointed at the teenager nearest to him. 'This is my daughter, Abbie, and her friend, Harriet.'

'Is Katie really dead?' Abbie glanced at Frankie through a long fringe.

'There has been no formal identification yet, but we believe it's her.'

'Do you mean you don't know for certain?' Harriet asked.

'I can't say more than that at the moment, not until the family has made a positive identification.'

Both girls were teary, causing Frankie to falter for a moment. He could humour most people, but teenage girls often got the better of him.

'Did you have a good party last night, Abigail?' he asked, hoping to put them at ease.

Abigail nodded. 'Yes, thanks. It was brilliant to see everyone.'

'And you invited Katie and Ethan?'

Abigail nodded again. 'I invited lots of friends from school and college, some who I hadn't seen in a while.'

'How was Katie? Did you get time to chat with her?'

He watched fleeting glances fly between the girls.

'She was dancing for most of the night,' Harriet said. 'We were all kinda merry.'

'Right. Was there any particular incident that stuck out to you during the evening?'

Fleeting glances again, and then they both shook their heads.

'It sounds like a great success.' He grinned. 'Whenever I went to parties at your age, there always seemed to be an argument or two.'

Both girls kept their eyes forwards this time, and he knew they were covering something up. He sat forwards. 'Whatever you're hiding, I need to know. There is camera footage that I can view, too.' He was fibbing after being told there was none. 'But I'd rather hear first-hand from you. We're all trying to find out who did this to Katie, so we need every possible lead.'

'She had an argument with Ethan,' Abigail said.

'Did you hear what about?'

'No, the music was too loud. All I saw were them shouting at each other. Ethan went to join his brother at the bar, and then Tommy Mason was chatting to Katie. Ethan went back and they left.'

Frankie stopped for a moment at the mention of Tommy Mason. He was the grandson of Liz Mason who he had interviewed earlier. He might be worth having a word with.

'What's Tommy like?'

'He's nice, a laugh.' Abigail smiled, a faint blush appearing on her cheeks.

Frankie spotted a crush going on there. 'So a lover's tiff, do you think?'

'Honestly don't know,' Harriet replied. 'It seemed something and nothing to be honest.'

'And there wasn't anything untoward going on with anyone else?'

They shook their heads vehemently.

Frankie put away his notebook and stood up. 'Okay, thanks for that, ladies. I'll be in touch if I need to know anything else. In the meantime, please be careful what you share on social media from the party last night.'

'Oh, there's not a lot. We took photos and a couple of videos.'

'Great. Could I borrow your phones so I can download the information? It could be very useful.'

'We need our phones.' Abigail's protests were weak under the circumstances, but he could hear annoyance creeping in.

'Okay then, how about you get your mum to make me a cup of tea and I'll have a flick through them both while I'm here?'

Frankie had them. They were reluctant to hand them over, but he promised to go through them quickly. That way he could decide if he needed to take them with him or not. He suspected most of the footage would be harmless fun, but who knew what might show itself as a result of someone not knowing they were being filmed or photographed.

CHAPTER TWENTY-ONE

Four months ago

After spending an hour together, Katie and Ethan were lying in his bed. There was no one home, but they didn't have to creep around anymore. Katie had stayed over for the past few Saturday nights, in the spare room. Either she or Ethan had snuck into each other when the house had been quiet. The first time had been awkward as she hadn't been able to keep quiet, getting a fit of the giggles, but once that was done, and she'd managed to get back to her room unnoticed, she relaxed a little.

Either way, it was much better to be there than at her home. It was a shame she couldn't return the favour. For starters, she only had a single bed and, to get to her room, they had to walk through Nate's. Shona used to be in there until Jacob moved in, so now she had the indignity of having to go through Nate's stinky mess before getting to bed.

So staying over with Ethan was bliss. But there was something she wanted to talk to him about.

'Your brother doesn't like me that much, does he?'

'What do you mean?' Ethan ran a finger lazily up and down her arm.

It made her shiver.

'I think he puts up with me, but he prefers it when I'm not around.'

'You're talking crap. He likes you. He told me.'

'But does he want us to be together for, well, you know, long enough to have a relationship?'

'Well, I do, and that's all that matters.'

'Really?' Katie propped herself up on her elbow and rested her head in her hand. It was the first time Ethan had said anything about an us.

'Yes, really. I like you, a lot.' He stopped for a moment. 'But I worry about what you might be getting yourself into. You know me and him do some dodgy shit and that our olds don't know about it. They'd ground us if they did.'

Ethan had shared a lot about his past with Katie. He'd told her how his granddad had built up the family business that his dad ran today and how it had been turned into an even bigger, more profitable company to pass on to his sons. However, neither Ethan nor Isaac wanted to be in the building trade and so were willing to do anything on the side to earn their money to escape it.

Ethan was quiet. Katie thought he was going to change his mind, but then he began.

'You do know the boxing club is a front?'

'A front for what?'

Ethan sighed.

Katie wasn't sure if he was annoyed with her or wary of what he was about to say.

'If I tell you something, you have to keep it to yourself,' he went on. 'We can make a lot of money if you do.'

'What do you mean?'

'You promise not to say anything? Not to anyone?'

'I promise.' Katie was already intrigued. She knew him and Isaac might be doing some illegal things as they were always in and out of the club and hanging around Flynn's. Was he trusting her with information? Her stomach flipped over.

'Well, there are three county lines run from the boxing club, plus local distribution. We deliver and pick up at the back of the building.'

Katie tried not to widen her eyes. Interested but wary at the same time, she wanted to know more. 'Is that why we have to go to the boxing club so often?'

'Yeah, and why I've left you to sit out in the car as I wasn't sure you'd want to be a part of it. But we could make a lot of money, transporting stuff around the country. The feds don't suspect a couple as much as people on their own. It's safer, too.'

'Are you saying you want me to come with you?'

'Only if you want to.'

'But what about Isaac?'

'I'll deal with him. He needs to know we can trust you. That's why he's so harsh on you at times. He's been testing you to see how you respond.'

'Well, I'm not happy about that.'

'But you can see why? We don't simply ask anyone to help out.'

Katie thought for a moment but then nodded. 'I'm not sure what I'm getting myself into, but if you'll look out for me?'

'Sure I will. Are you cool to do a run and see how you feel? It's only as far as Birmingham, Manchester, or Sheffield. Sometimes I have to go to London, but that's not too often.'

'Okay, let's do it. I need some excitement in my life.'

Ethan pushed her gently onto her back and climbed on top of her. 'Excitement, you say?' He ran a tongue across his upper lip. 'I can give you more of what we've just been up to if you want some right now?'

He kissed her again and Katie relaxed into it, certain that he'd keep her safe. She was thrilled to be invited into the firm and beyond excited to learn more.

How cool was all this after only seeing Ethan for two months? She wouldn't let him down.

CHAPTER TWENTY-TWO

Sam Markham yawned as she made her way out of the station. It had been an unexpected long day, exhausting and emotional, too. She couldn't wait to get home and see her daughter. Not so much her husband, Craig.

For the past few months, they'd been having problems, and Sam wasn't sure if she wanted to continue with her marriage or call it a day. She and Craig had been together for fifteen years, but there was more to life than awkward silences, space between sheets, and a mostly platonic relationship.

Yet at times like these, she realised how important family was. Her heart went out to Donna Frost who, without her husband, would have to suffer the brunt of the family's grief. Keeping them together, holding them close while they mourned. It never failed to amaze Sam how resilient people were when it came to getting on with things for the dignity of a deceased one.

She checked her phone for messages. There were four. One from her daughter, asking what time she'd be home. Two from Craig asking the same, and one from Aaron.

Sam never thought she'd start an affair. She was always the sensible one, stating that people should finish one relationship before embarking on another. But when it came down to it, she had fallen for Aaron so quickly it had made her realise how things like that really did just happen.

Aaron was a traffic cop. He did shifts, so their paths didn't cross much. But one night after a hectic day and evening, Sam had been leaving the station when her car wouldn't start. Aaron had finished his shift and offered to help, and when he couldn't do anything about the problem, he sat and waited with her for the breakdown company to arrive. They'd had a natter, sharing a coffee from a flask that had been prepared so long ago the liquid was tepid.

When the recovery truck had turned up, Sam hadn't wanted the evening to end. She'd never laughed so much in the company of a man for ages, and it had warmed her heart.

Aaron waved her off, and she thought that would be the end of it. But they kept bumping into each other. Soon they were having the odd coffee or lunch in the canteen, then a quick drink at Chimneys next door.

One night they'd had a drink too many and caught a taxi home together. While they waited for it to arrive, Sam had been in such a good mood, and when Aaron moved to kiss her, she drew him close.

That was four months ago. Four months of sneaking around, leading a double life, wanting to get out of one and step into another permanently.

But it wasn't all about her. There was Emily to think of as well as her husband. Craig could cope, but was it fair to put her daughter through it all? She'd obviously stay with Sam, which would make things awkward with childcare, often shared between both grandmothers whenever necessary.

But there had to be a suitable solution because she couldn't go on like this. Aaron was divorced and had his own place. He was forever asking her to move in with him, but she couldn't uproot Emily, not into someone else's home. It was a delicate line between upsetting her and yet being unhappy herself. So far, there had been no easy way out.

The sight of a cheeky message Aaron had sent earlier made her smile. She had her head down replying to it and almost missed the large brown envelope pushed under the windscreen wiper on the driver's side. She reached for it, noticing it had no writing on it.

She grinned, expecting it to be something silly from Aaron. But instead she found photos of the two of them. There was one in the pub, one in the car park here. There was even one at the end of her street when Aaron had dropped her off one evening and she'd then got into her own car. They weren't explicit but they were damning.

There was also a note, written on lined paper. In black ink and capitals it said: THERE'S NO PLACE LIKE HOME.

Sam pushed it back in the envelope with the photos and shoved it into her bag. Someone had seen them. Ohmigod! Her blood drained at the thought.

She glanced around, to see if anyone was watching now, waiting for her reaction. But of course she could see no one. Who in their right mind would do that anyway?

Then again, who had been observing her in the first place? And why? It was no one's business but her own.

Was it Craig? Had he found out and this was the only way he could tell her?

She drove home, exhaustion overtaken by anxiety now. As she parked her car in the drive, she took a moment. The house was welcoming, curtains open, and she could see into the living room from where she was. Craig was lying flat out on the settee. Emily would obviously be in bed by now, the lamp in her bedroom glowing.

Would Craig be able to sleep so easily if he'd put that

envelope on her car? Surely he'd be waiting with interest to see what she said when she arrived home.

Was it someone at work, who had seen her and Aaron together? But why the note? It was a well-known fact with their role that there were so many affairs between work colleagues. After all, they spent more time there than at home.

God, what was she going to do? Say nothing and hope it blew over? But if it wasn't Craig, who would it be?

Eventually, she went in. She closed the door quietly and removed her coat and shoes. Craig was stretching his arms above his head when she stepped inside the living room. He swivelled round until his feet were on the floor.

'You seem knackered,' he said, running a hand through his hair. 'Want a brew?'

'I'd love one, ta,' she replied.

And just like that, Sam realised it wasn't Craig. He wouldn't be able to look her in the eye, deny knowledge of what he'd done.

It left her with another dilemma when guilt overtook her. She had to tell Craig soon, or end things with Aaron. Having the best of both worlds was not what she'd intended doing, and it wasn't fair on either of them. And let's face it, being there with Craig seemed to be her favoured plan B.

But right now she didn't know how to react to someone being out to get her, never mind clear her conscience dealing with the men in her life.

CHAPTER TWENTY-THREE

After catching up on a few things at the station, Allie was home at last. It was quite early for the first day of a murder investigation, but as everything was mostly talking to people, and the press release hadn't gone out yet, there was a limit to what they could do without interrupting everyday life around the crime scene.

So at half past ten, Allie found both Mark and Poppy in the living room at either end of the settee. Dexter, who had come to greet her at the door, followed her in, sitting on the floor by Poppy's feet.

Poppy had clearly been asleep, her hair a mess of blonde wisps. Mark was watching a TV reality show, which Allie knew meant he'd fallen asleep too and it had come on without his knowledge. It was sweet of them both to wait up for her, though.

'Hey, guys.' Allie sat down between them.

'How's your day been?' Mark asked.

'Long and tiring. And you?' She glanced at Poppy. 'Did you miss me?'

'Of course not.'

Allie smiled and pulled Poppy into her arms. The young girl was already falling asleep again.

Allie turned to see Mark's eyes were closed, too. She laughed inwardly. If only she could switch off so quickly. She sat contemplating the day until the break came on.

'I heard about that girl, Allie,' Poppy spoke quietly. 'I hope she wasn't in pain for very long.'

'Me, too, Pops.' Allie kept her voice steady, not wanting to alarm Poppy.

'Are the family okay?'

'It's hard to lose any brother or sister,' Allie replied. 'I still feel a part of me is missing every day, and I know you feel that way about your mum.'

At twenty-five, Allie's older sister, Karen, had been attacked and left for dead. Allie had been fifteen minutes late collecting her after a night out. That was all it had taken. The perpetrator was caught eventually, but Karen never fully recovered. She'd needed twenty-four-hour care and had died ten years ago.

When they'd first met Poppy, her mum had been dying of a brain tumour. There was no one to look after her while she was in hospital, and so they'd gone through the grieving process with her. It had helped that Allie had Karen to mention every now and again.

Poppy had stayed with them ever since. That had been nearly a year ago, and no one wanted her to leave. It was something she and Mark had started discussing, whether to adopt Poppy. Their main aim had been to foster, but then again, they'd probably always dreamed of meeting a child who would steal their heart.

Family.

Allie still got a kick from fostering, but it would be nice to adopt one or two children. Having older kids suited them better than the younger ones, she suspected, but she and

Mark would give a home to whoever needed it, no matter the age.

Allie nudged Mark. 'Come on, you, time for bed.'

'Has the film finished, Pops?'

'What film?' Allie scoffed. 'There was crass reality TV on when I came home.'

'That's outrageous. We don't watch that kind of thing in this house.' Mark yawned and stretched his hands over his head. 'Which reminds me, when is the next episode of *Celebrity Hunted* airing?'

Allie pulled Poppy to her feet, laughing. 'I leave you alone for one evening.'

'Night,' Poppy said, leaning down to kiss Mark.

'Night, duck. I'll be up soon to check on you,' Mark told her.

Allie beamed. It was all so wonderful to come home to after a crappy day.

Yet once in bed, it took her a while to settle. It was important to see her loved ones were safe after the murder of Katie Frost. Being with her family grounded Allie. Yet her thoughts returned to the day's events, wondering how the Frost family were coping that evening.

It had been truly heartbreaking to see them crumble when she'd told them the news first thing. Still, her team were on it. There was much to look into tomorrow, check, cross-reference.

Someone wouldn't be telling the truth, and it was up to them to search for the real answers.

SUNDAY - DAY TWO

CHAPTER TWENTY-FOUR

Even though it was close to one a.m. when Allie finally got to sleep, she was up and out of the house for seven. During the car journey to the station, she thought about the woman yesterday who had stumbled across Katie Frost's body about the same time.

The morning was cool but fresh, and she wondered what the day would bring. It was going to be an emotional one.

First visit was to the mortuary to allow the family to identify Katie Frost's body. Then there would be a press conference and the deluge of work that brought with it. As well, the police hotline was twenty-four-seven, so maybe there might be a call from a witness or an anonymous tip-off to respond to that had come in overnight.

It had been lovely to spend time with Mark and Poppy last night, although not so much thinking about Karen. Katie Frost was eight years younger than Allie's sister, Karen, was when she was attacked, yet whoever had murdered Katie was still out there. Until then, Allie wouldn't stop until the killer was behind bars. People in her city deserved to feel safe when they went out and about.

She was the first one in at the station but was quickly followed by Frankie and Sam. When Frankie had made drinks for everyone, Allie joined them in the main room, sitting on the edge of Sam's desk. As she was about to start without Perry, he came rushing in, his tie hanging around his neck undone.

'Perry! Wonderful of you to join us,' Allie teased, motioning for him to sit down quickly.

'Sorry, boss.' He glanced at everyone in turn. 'My boy has been vomiting all night.'

'Oh, the poor lamb,' Allie commiserated. 'How is he now?'

'I was about to come out when he decided he'd throw up all over me.' Perry retched. 'I hope I'm not too whiffy. I can still smell it.'

'Well, I can't, so you'll do. We were about to go through PM results before I shoot off to do the ID on Katie Frost's body with her family. Nothing new has come in overnight, we're still waiting on forensics, and there are plenty of actions to follow up on. Oh, I need you to stand in for me at the press conference this morning.' Perry was about to protest when Allie held up a hand. 'You only have to sit pretty and report back to me. Jenny is taking it.'

'I bloody hope that's all. You're way better at dealing with journos than me. It freaks me out when I'm asked anything. Everything I shouldn't say runs through my head, stopping me from saying what I need to!'

'You'll be fine. I learned a lot by observing her. She's very calm and collected, until she's on her own.' Allie grinned, then turned to look around the room. 'There is nothing of interest for us from the PM, I'm afraid. It is as we thought. Death was caused by blunt force trauma. But it wasn't with a sharp object. It seems to have been a fist, or a slap and then a push, possibly a backhander, that knocked her off her feet and she landed heavily on the ground, cracking her skull on the row of edging stones before the grass. There was blood on it. Had she landed a few inches further back, there is a likelihood she might have survived as she would have hit soil, and as we've had a lot of rain lately, it was quite muddy, not hard ground.'

'Oh, no, that's so sad,' Sam said, everyone murmuring their agreement.

'And obviously gives us no chance to find a murder weapon with forensics on it, linking the victim and the suspect. There aren't any signs of sexual assault either, thankfully. It seems as if she sustained some injuries when her shoe came off when she was dragged out of sight as some of the skin on the bottom of her left foot is missing and covered in mud and gravel. Other than that, there is no evidence to link her to anyone.'

'So it's the usual waiting game,' Perry chirped up.

'I'm afraid so. I'll let you know what Dave says once his report is back, but if he draws a blank, which is possible, then we won't move from square one. Let's keep our fingers crossed for some further forensics once more tests are complete.' Allie glanced at the list on her phone to see if there was anything else to mention. 'Ah, Rachel, FLO, gave me a quick update. She managed to chat with Beth, Katie's best friend. She said she'd seen her with a lot of money lately.'

'Maybe she had a recent birthday?' Frankie commented.

'She asked her that, and she said no. Katie said Ethan had given it to her to treat herself. Rachel thought Beth was talking about no more than the odd note here and there, so I asked the search team to see if they could find anything. They didn't. Also, they'd both recently finished working at somewhere they felt harassed.' Allie told them about the shopkeeper's son. 'I'll get uniform to have a word, check out where this guy was et cetera. He needs someone to warn him off regardless. Creepy git.' She scrolled down the screen on her phone and then looked up. 'Okay, let's get to it, folks.'

CHAPTER TWENTY-FIVE

Hannah knocked on Beth's bedroom door before opening it. Two mugs of hot chocolate were in one hand, and she was doing a further balancing act with a packet of biscuits under her arm.

'I thought you might like these,' she said, spotting her daughter lying on her stomach on the bed, her laptop open.

'Thanks, Mum.' Beth wriggled across to her, took both drinks and popped them on the bedside cabinet.

Hannah sat on the edge of the bed and passed her the biscuits. 'How are you feeling today?'

'Lost.'

Hannah noticed Beth's eyes were red and swollen. She wished there was something she could do to ease her pain. Beth and Katie had been mostly joined at the hip until the last couple of weeks, which was something she wished she'd asked about before. Usually they fell out for a few hours, sometimes a day or so, but never that long.

'Why did you and Katie argue?' Hannah ventured. 'Was it about Ethan?'

Beth shrugged. 'She was spending more time with him

than me. It was bound to happen one day. But I wished it hadn't been him.'

'Why not?'

'He wasn't right for her.'

'Sometimes we don't choose who we fall in love with. We find out when it's too late that we're incompatible. I should know, I married your dad.'

'Mum!'

Hannah laughed. Beth knew she was joking. She and Wes had been together nigh on twenty years. They had their ups and downs like any married couple with kids, but they were solid.

'So Ethan wasn't... rough with Katie at any time?'

'I don't think so. Why?'

'Nothing really. I wondered if he'd been kind to her. She deserved that after losing her dad at such a young age.'

'Ethan was...'

The stop made Hannah frown. 'Was what?'

'Nothing.' Beth tore open the biscuits and took a bite from one before handing the packet to her. 'Want one before I demolish the pack?'

Hannah smiled, knowing when she was being given the brush-off. Maybe Beth would tell her things in her own time, but for now she wouldn't push her.

'I wanted to check to see how you are really. I know it can't be easy for you, but at least you have us. You know you can talk to me or your dad about anything if you need to.'

'Yeah, I do, Mum.'

Hannah left her then, glad that her family were all so supportive of one another.

CHAPTER TWENTY-SIX

Shona sat up in bed and swung her legs round to the floor. She rubbed the base of her back for a moment and then lifted herself to standing. Her bump was getting bigger by the day now, and she was counting down the weeks and days to her due date in two months' time.

She always found it hard to sleep on her back, yet it was the only way she could get comfortable now. Jacob had been no help as he'd lain beside her snoring. Honestly, there could be a crash outside their window, and he wouldn't hear a thing. Shona wished she was the same instead of constantly worrying about the arrival of their daughter.

'Morning, little one.' She placed a hand on her stomach. 'I hope you had a better night's sleep than me.'

In the corner of the room stood a wicker Moses basket on a stand. Pink blankets and bedding were piled high inside it, ready for when she brought Olivia home. That was the name she and Jacob had chosen, plus now with Katie as a middle name. She couldn't wait to see her daughter, get to know her and bring her up properly.

The bed beside her was empty, which was unusual because

it was only half past eight. Pushing her feet into her slippers, she trundled into the bathroom. It was such an effort to do anything these days, feeling like a beached whale, so she took a shower rather than lounge in the bath.

She was so tired. She'd hardly slept the night before, thinking about Katie. Every time she'd closed her eyes, her sister's face popped up and she would find herself crying. But she knew she had to look after herself at the moment. She needed to keep her strength up.

Shona hadn't planned on having a baby so young, and especially not long into a relationship with Jacob. After seeing what it had done to her mum, having three so close together, she'd wanted to live her life before being tied down with a child. But even though she and Jacob had been careful to use protection, there'd been the odd lapse when they'd come back from The Fox and Hare. She wasn't proud of herself.

When she'd found out she was pregnant, she hadn't wanted to tell Jacob straightaway. He'd guessed after three bouts of morning sickness and had been delighted at the news. Shona couldn't help feeling proud of him now. He wanted to do a better job than his dad had with him, which wasn't hard as he'd been a mean bastard, but she didn't voice that to him.

She and Jacob had met at Flynn's. They'd been together for nearly two years now. Jacob was a year older than her, but more often than not, he acted like he was a lot younger. She couldn't understand at times why he took orders from someone further up the chain, when he had what was needed to be a player. Still, at least he was working as well.

Since she'd announced she was having a baby, Shona had grown closer to her mum, too, and she'd been looking forward to having her sister there to help out. Katie had been so excited waiting to meet her niece.

After her shower, she was on her way back to her room when she passed the door leading to Katie's bedroom. She pushed the handle, walked through Nate's bedroom and into her sister's.

It still smelt of her, causing her to catch her breath. She sat down on her bed and glanced around. She recalled sitting there lots of times listening to Katie talking about things as she'd grown up – toys, games, magazines, music, more recently makeup and boys. She had loved having a younger sister to chat with.

She spotted a gym bag. Pulling out a T-shirt, she lifted it to her nose and inhaled Katie's scent. It was a tough reminder, but she couldn't put it down, squeezing her eyes shut to stop more tears.

Once steady again, she wanted to know what else was in there. It was a pile of dirty washing really, but neither she nor her mum would be able to clean it for a while. Seeing a lipstick she knew was Katie's favourite colour, she took it for herself. She would be reminded of her whenever she applied it. Lady Pink: it had the perfect name for her little sister.

Then she reached for the small white teddy Ethan had bought Katie a while ago. She checked its pocket, recalling a conversation about the memory stick she'd found tucked inside the toy's trousers. She searched for it, but it wasn't there.

She pocketed the lipstick and, keeping hold of the teddy, pushed herself up to standing again. She'd keep it for the baby. It would be something to remind her of the aunty she would never get to meet.

A last glance around, with a sigh. One day soon, they would have to pack up everything in the room and decide what to do with it. Most of it could go to a charity, the furniture to a homeless one, perhaps.

A selfish thought came to mind. It might be better now if

she and Jacob moved into Nate's room, and the baby could have Katie's. It would be quieter for the rest of the family, and Katie could be close to her then. Shona believed in the afterlife and knew her sister would watch over the baby.

She had to believe that. It was the only way she could get through each day.

Jacob was in the kitchen with Nate and Donna when she finally got downstairs.

'Morning, love. Tea?' Donna asked as she pulled out a chair for her.

'That would be nice, ta.' Shona lowered herself into it. 'Is there any news?'

'No, duck. Rachel is in the living room. She's been here for about an hour already. We'll be ready to go to the mortuary soon.'

'I want to come with you.'

'Are you sure? You didn't want to yesterday, and I'll—'

'No, I want to now.'

'I might try and put together the cot this afternoon,' Jacob suggested. 'Something to cheer us all up.'

'Great!' Shona was enthusiastic about that. She'd been asking him for a couple of weeks now and had thought she'd have to do it herself.

'I'll help him, too,' Nate offered. 'It'll keep my mind occupied.'

Shona glanced over, first at her brother and then Jacob. Why were they being so nice all of a sudden? She hoped it didn't have anything to do with what they'd been doing on Friday night.

Because, even without the visit to the mortuary, they were lying to her about something.

CHAPTER TWENTY-SEVEN

Four months ago

As soon as Ethan beeped the car horn outside the house, Katie rushed downstairs and grabbed her coat. Her mum came out of the living room.

'Going somewhere nice?' she asked.

'Out for a drink. I might stay at Ethan's tonight, so don't wait up.'

'When am I going to meet him? It's been weeks now. I can't think why you're hiding him from me.'

'Let me speak to him about coming over this weekend? Perhaps you can do a Sunday roast?'

Mum nodded. 'Okay, that will be nice. I'm looking forward to seeing him.'

'You'll love him.' Katie beamed with pride. A horn beeped again, and she rushed to the door. 'Bye, Mum. Laters!'

She got in the car, leaned over to kiss Ethan, and buckled up. 'So where are we going?'

'Manchester.'

'Cool, it will be a nice ride in this motor.'

'We're catching the train from Stoke.'

'Oh. I thought—'

'I used the car last week. Have to alternate the ways we travel and the routes so as not to create a pattern.'

'I suppose it makes sense to be careful.'

Twenty minutes later, they were on the train chatting nineteen to the dozen. Conversation with Ethan had flowed well for the most part, as long as she didn't talk about things he might get jealous over. Once she mentioned a trip to Scotland with Beth and her family. Beth's brother, Mitchell, had a crush on her when she was fifteen. He'd grown out of it now, and it had been funny at the time.

But because Ethan knew Mitchell, he wasn't best pleased. He'd sulked for quite some time and made a comment about sloppy seconds. They'd fallen out then. She'd told him how hurt she was, but they made up later and he'd apologised. Which was good because she hadn't slept with Mitchell, nor would she ever.

Ethan was fine again after that. Katie thought he'd liked her showing spirit and sticking up for herself. She did like a bad boy but also knew she'd have to hold her own if Ethan was going to treat her well. Some girls could be pushovers. She wasn't one of them.

It didn't take long for the train to arrive at Manchester Piccadilly, and they got a cab to a bar not far from Canal Street. Ethan had a holdall over his shoulder, and Katie knew he had either drugs or cash in it. Part of her was excited, the thrill of doing something illegal outdoing the nerves running through her body at the thought of getting caught.

A man came into the bar and straight over to Ethan. He sat with them for a few minutes, and then they both went outside. Katie was told to follow them after ten minutes.

Time seemed to stretch out as she tapped her fingers to the beat of the music against her empty glass, looking as if she was having fun while she waited for her partner to come back.

When she finally got outside, Ethan was leaning on the wall and scrolling down his phone.

'Everything okay?' Katie asked.

Ethan grinned and put an arm around her shoulder. 'Top notch,' he said as they walked away.

The trip back on the train went without a hitch. They got into his car and headed to the boxing club. Once Ethan had dropped off his stash, the evening was theirs. It was half past nine.

Ethan passed her a few notes. 'One hundred quid,' he said.

'What's that for?'

'Your fee for coming along.'

'But I didn't do anything.'

'Runners get paid. It might not be as easy as it was this time.'

'What do you mean?'

'If we get caught...'

'Oh.' Katie wasn't sure she wanted to know about that part.

'Fun to take a risk, though? And if you're nabbed first time, you'll only get a warning.'

'Have you ever been?'

'Nope.'

She thought about it. Was it really too much of a risk? But then, she was seventeen, going out with Ethan and living her best life. What was not to like? Sure, she knew it was dangerous, but if it was true what Ethan said, that the cops were lenient on anyone caught for the first time, then it was worth it.

Wasn't it?

CHAPTER TWENTY-EIGHT

Allie disliked going to the mortuary with murder victims' relatives but knew it was an imperative part of her job. She could also gauge how family members were feeling by their reactions, although some had fooled her in the past due to their grief. People could be in a state of shock and not come across as their best. She'd had relatives crying on her shoulder, and tried always to be compassionate, but she had a job to do. Asking difficult questions was often offensive to grieving relatives. She'd even had a slap across the face from one, through no fault of her own.

She'd taken Frankie with her that morning. They arrived half an hour before the Frost family, being driven there by the family liaison officer. It was a time to catch up with Rachel, too, see if she had learned anything new.

As they drank a quick coffee in the office, Allie read through Simon's feature on Katie's murder for *Stoke News*. It concentrated on the tragedy of a girl found metres from the safety of her home, the affect it would have on family, friends, and neighbours, and the wider community. It had a short interview with Donna, and a couple of girls who Allie read were Katie's friends. Simon must have spoken to them around the crime scene yesterday. As ever, he'd been sensitive and diplomatic.

Her phone alerted her to a message.

'They're here.' She stood up.

'Is it the same no matter what the age?' Frankie enquired when they made their way through to the reception area.

'For me, the younger the victim, the harder it is, but they are all dead because of someone else, no matter what.' Allie opened a door and held it for Frankie to go through. 'It's something I never get used to. But you can sometimes learn a lot from a victim's relatives or friends, so I always try and attend.'

In the reception area, the family were waiting. Allie noticed the deathly colour of Donna Frost immediately. She looked as if she hadn't slept a wink the night before – no doubt she hadn't. Shona was holding on to her arm, Nate and Jacob either side of them. Allie nodded at Rachel who was standing behind them, hands entwined in front of her.

'Morning, how are you feeling?' Allie asked. It seemed a stupid question, but personal small talk often put the families at ease.

'Still shellshocked,' Donna replied for them all. 'We want to get this over with. It won't seem real until we do.'

Allie felt for her. There was no easy way to identify a murdered teenager.

'We'll go into a room where there will be a glass panel on the wall. It will be covered with curtains, and once you're ready, they will be opened, and Katie will be lying on a trolley. You won't be able to see any injuries on her, and only her head will be showing regardless. Please don't worry about anything else.' She indicated to a door at the side. 'If you'd like to follow me.'

They all went ahead, and Allie spoke directly to Donna. 'Ready?' she queried.

Donna nodded, and the curtain was drawn back. The cry that came from her was like the sound of an animal in pain. She almost dropped to the floor as her knees gave way, but Nate held on to her.

'Is that Katie?' Allie had to ask.

'Yes, yes. Oh, why is it her?' Donna sobbed.

Shona was crying, too; they hugged each other for comfort. Nate was openly weeping, Jacob trying not to.

'Would you like some time alone with her?'

Donna shook her head and then nodded. 'Please.'

Allie and Frankie left them in the room with a mortuary assistant.

Frankie blew out a long breath. 'That was intense. I had to hold my own tears back.'

'Believe me, I've cried several times over the years. Don't be afraid to show your emotions. We're only human.'

'How awful for them. She's so young.'

Rachel was sitting in the reception area, scrolling through her phone. She closed it quickly when she saw them and stood up.

'Anything for us?' Allie asked when they drew level.

'Nothing new. How was it?'

'Awful but necessary. I suppose until they see her, it doesn't sink in.'

'Donna did ask when she would get Katie's possessions back. She mentioned a necklace, a heart-shaped pendant that she'd bought Katie for her sixteenth birthday.'

Allie frowned. 'I'd have to check but I don't think there was one.' She got out her phone, slipped outside and rang Sam. 'Can you find out if Katie had any jewellery on her, please? We've had the body ID'd formally, too.'

'Right. Hang on. No, there's no mention of a necklace, a bracelet, nor a ring.'

'Interesting. We're heading back to the station now, so I'll catch up with you then.'

Allie disconnected the call and stood for a moment. Where was the necklace? Had Katie forgotten to put it on and perhaps Donna would find it once she got home? Or if not, had their killer taken it, as a trophy? She shuddered suddenly. She hated that kind of thing. Not only did a murderer find pleasure in the kill, but they then took mementoes?

She went back inside to find the Frost family had come out of the side room. Allie kept her thoughts to herself for now, wanting to do some digging beforehand, hoping to save the family more pain. But it would have to be dealt with. If there was no necklace found, who had taken it?

CHAPTER TWENTY-NINE

Allie parked up as near to the crime scene as she could. It was quarter to six, and the place was teeming with people. Most of them were teenagers, Katie's friends, she presumed, and others who had heard the news. Anything like this touched a lot of people, and not just around the immediate area. And even though there were people of all ages in the crowd, there was almost a solidarity of silence, too. Quiet little huddles of conversations, a few sobs here and there, but nothing above that.

Since they'd found Katie's body yesterday, it had been slow going trying to piece together her last known movements. Everything was coming in, but there were no leads as to who had attacked her. This was always the monotonous part of the job, the waiting, the trawling, the viewing. Conversations with members of the public. Analysing movements, going over and checking out information.

'Right, gang.' Allie looked at each one of them in turn. Perry, Frankie, and Sam were with her. 'You know what to do. Be mindful of not appearing too pushy for information but keep eyes and ears peeled. You know how many times suspects have come to these kinds of things. They could be among the throng, if so.'

Sam and Frankie, who were sitting in the back, nodded.

'Shall I stay with the family, too, boss?' Perry, in the passenger seat beside her, asked.

'Yes, I think that's wise. I want to see if anything goes on between Nate and Jacob. I have a niggle after seeing them earlier, a feeling they're lying about something. Whether or not it's linked to this case remains to be seen, but if I see them alone, I'm going to try and listen in.'

Once out of the car, Allie moved around a group of girls who were comforting each other. They were all holding paper copies of an image of Katie, one which had been shared with the media half an hour ago.

Perry nudged her and pointed in the distance, where a camera crew were setting up. It was a positive they were here, she supposed. Media outlets were always a double-edged sword in their role. But Sam would be able to scrutinise the footage tomorrow and see if she spotted anything out of the ordinary.

No matter what, for the family, it would feel intrusive.

'Had any plans for this evening, boss?' Perry asked as they walked along Carlisle Street.

'None whatsoever. I was feeling the pain after three nights out on the trot.'

'Old-timer.'

All private conversation was halted as they knocked on the Frost's front door. Allie was pleased to see Rachel opened it, letting them in.

'How are things?' she asked in almost a whisper.

'Quiet,' Rachel replied. 'Donna and Shona have mostly been sitting around looking at photos, TV on mute in the background, except for watching the news conference. Nate and Jacob have been building the cot upstairs, so there's been a little laughter and tears with that.'

Allie understood that. Sometimes after a murder, relatives didn't know how to react. Things would never be normal again for the Frost family. Even though they knew Katie had died, they would still be in denial, expecting her to walk through the door at any minute.

They went through to the living room where the family were gathered.

'Do you want to leave from the front of the house or the back?' Allie checked with Donna.

'I think we'll go out the back. I can walk alone with my thoughts while I prepare myself.'

'I suspect the press may be lurking around. You don't have to speak to them. I will usher you past and tell them to show some respect if they expect too much.'

Once coats were on, and flowers in hands ready to be laid, Allie and Rachel led the family out. Shona clung on to Donna, Nate and Jacob following behind. Perry brought up the rear.

There were several neighbours standing at their gates, each having the dignity to stay silent as they passed. Allie could hear sniffles coming from Shona. It brought back memories of when she'd done the same, clinging on to her mum for comfort, blanketed in disbelief and guilt over what had happened to her own sister.

It was a poignant moment when they came onto the road in full view of everyone. There were people everywhere along the pavement and grouped together by the edge of the fields. Several police in uniform had been drafted in to stop the public trampling around the edges of the crime scene, but even with such a huge crowd, everyone was showing respect. She hoped it stayed that way.

Allie heard Donna gasp and turned to see her a little unsteady on her feet.

'If at any time you find this too much, please let me know,' she said, her voice a tad shaky with emotion. She looked at Donna, clearing her throat and regaining her composure. A moment of understanding passed between them.

'No, I have to do this.' Donna pulled herself up tall and walked ahead.

CHAPTER THIRTY

Donna couldn't stop shaking when she walked through the parting crowd. All eyes were on her and her family. She had never wanted to be invisible so much in her life.

It was wonderful of all these people to come out in support, grieving for Katie, but she didn't want to be a part of it. In her mind, this wasn't happening. She would go to bed that evening and wake up tomorrow with the weekend as a memory of a bad dream.

Her little girl couldn't be gone. Who would do such a thing?

She kept her eyes to the front at first, unable to meet anyone else's eye. Then, she spotted a neighbour who gave her a watery smile, and she realised again how important it was for her to do what was right to catch the person who had ripped out another huge part of their family.

In her pocket, her phone vibrated. She took it out quickly to see a message from Woody. He was asking if the police had any news. Although Donna knew he was being kind to stay in touch, she didn't have time for him. Her family were her priority, so she put the phone away.

Her bottom lip trembled as she got to the nearest place to the cordon. Rows and rows of floral tributes, teddy bears, and candles went as far as the eye could see. Donna recognised some of the girls who were huddled in groups, crying, comforting each other.

Then she froze. She hoped people weren't waiting for her to speak to them. She couldn't do that.

But when she stopped, no one bothered her, or the family. They walked along the line, bending to read messages of tribute to Katie.

A few minutes went by, and she thought she'd be able to hold in her tears, but one particular message broke her. It was from her neighbour at number twenty-eight.

A part of the street has been torn away. I will miss you, Katie. Shine bright in the sky. Liz Mason.

Next to it was a single rose, wrapped in cellophane. *RIP, Katie. Miss you, Tommy.*

Donna moved away after that, unable to see through her tears. At half past six, music would begin to play, and everyone had been told to let their balloons go. It would be a surreal moment, one she never thought she'd be a part of, but it would be a beautiful tribute to the young girl who'd never turn into a woman.

Never get married.

Never have her own children and grandchildren.

Never see her brother and sister grow up.

Never do anything but rot in a grave where she didn't belong.

Donna dropped to her knees and sobbed. She didn't care who was watching. All she wanted was her daughter back.

CHAPTER THIRTY-ONE

Allie stood to one side as the family addressed the crowd, her team by her side. To all intents and purposes, a police presence was necessary for support or if anyone stepped out of line, which had happened on occasions before at these kinds of events when emotions overrun.

But so far everything had gone well. It seemed as if the whole community was grieving the loss of Katie Frost, and it was nice to see, whether or not they knew the young woman. Any life taken tragically brought out a crowd. When it was near, or in the vicinity of where you lived, it shocked that little bit more.

Once Donna had composed herself, the family had lit candles and read sympathy messages that had been left on the flowers close to the crime scene tape. People began to disperse. Some stayed behind, mixing in different groups, and it was these who Allie and her team hoped to infiltrate.

'Let's split up,' Allie told them, glancing at her watch. 'One hour will do it and then we can grab a drink at the station to compare notes.'

She watched Perry, Sam, and Frankie walk off in different

directions. Allie chatted to the people closest to her for a while and then made her way to others. A young girl crying in the arms of an older woman caught her eye, and she headed over.

'I'm so sorry for your loss,' Allie said, holding up her warrant card. 'I don't want to intrude, but we're trying to find out as much as we can about Katie.' She looked at the younger woman. 'Did you know her well?'

'She... she was my best friend.' Her words brought more tears.

'Ah, it's Beth, isn't it? Rachel spoke to you yesterday.'

She nodded, her mother giving a sympathetic squeeze.

'She was a lovely girl,' she told Allie.

'Do you live local?'

'Yes, at the far end of the street, number forty-two. I'm Hannah Lightwood. We've known the family since they moved here when Beth and Katie were in junior school.'

Allie grimaced, knowing what it would be like for Beth. At that age, friendships were everything, and she imagined she'd feel like a part of her was missing for a long time to come, very similar to her situation with her sister, Karen. All the secrets they would have shared about boys and dating, the clothes they would have borrowed from each other. The laughs, the tantrums, the pure joy of adolescence.

She got out her notebook. 'You say you live at number forty-two?'

'Yes. There's me and my husband, Wes, who had to go into work this evening, and my son, Mitchell.' She glanced around and beckoned to someone.

Two young men walked over to them.

Hannah indicated the one on the left. 'That's my lad, Mitchell.' She pointed to the other. 'And Tommy, lives at number twenty-eight Park Avenue.'

Allie introduced herself. She asked them a few general

questions about Katie and then let them go on their way. She could see they were anxious to get back to their friends. Beth went with them.

'Katie has been a bit unruly lately,' Hannah said quietly, once they were out of hearing range. 'I was worried about Beth, to be truthful. I didn't want anything to rub off on her, but I think Katie has been led astray by her boyfriend.'

'Oh?'

'Beth is guarded about what she's saying. I've tried to talk to her about it, but she's being loyal to Katie.' Hannah hesitated. 'I don't think she has anything concrete, just a feeling, you know?'

'Hmm, okay.' Allie glanced around to see where Ethan Riley and his family were. She'd seen them earlier but couldn't spot them now.

Hannah lowered her voice to an almost whisper. 'I think the family fell apart a bit when Max died, if I'm honest.'

Allie gave a faint smile of acknowledgement. She didn't like anyone passing judgment on people's circumstances, but in her job it was par for the course. Everything anyone told them could turn out to be gossip or lies to throw them off the scent of something else, or it could be the truth. Pinch of salt and all that. And her job to sort out the wheat from the chaff.

Seeing Simon, she made her way through the crowd towards him. He waved when he saw her and came over.

'It's a decent turnout, even though sad,' he said to her as they met halfway.

'It is. It's always harder the younger the victim, too. To get your head around why, to understand, to imagine. How are you? Heard anything useful?'

'Not yet, I don't think.' Simon threw a thumb over his shoulder. 'I was chatting to a group of girls over there, but unless I go for the jugular and ask if anyone didn't like Katie, then it's all good stuff about her.'

'Don't ever change, Simon.' She smiled faintly. 'Not like that Lawrence tosser. He isn't known for his tact. I haven't seen him here, have you?'

'No, which is unusual, but I'll take it.'

'Excellent! Let's hope he's washing his hair.'

A while later, Donna was still in shock mode, but her tears had dried a little. She'd been wandering around, talking to people, giving and receiving hugs and words of comfort. Everyone was being so nice, but all she wanted to do was go home and curl up in a dark room.

She glanced at her watch, wondering when it would be polite to leave. She'd been there an hour and half, every one of those minutes painful. Perhaps it wouldn't seem too bad if she slipped off now.

Suddenly from behind her, she heard a kerfuffle. The sounds of shouting rose, and she turned in time to see Nate launch himself at Isaac Riley. Isaac dodged the fist that was coming his way as his friends tried to drag Nate away.

'I'm going to knock your head off if I find out you have anything to do with this,' he yelled.

'I wouldn't do that,' Isaac replied. 'So you'd better stop spreading rumours about—'

'You were jealous of Ethan. Everyone knows.'

Isaac shook his head, but there was a menacing look appearing on his face. One that Donna recognised as "don't push me." She raced over to the group and put herself in the middle of them. Ruth Riley did the same. The mothers faced each other's son.

'What's going on?' Donna wanted to know.

'Ask him,' Nate cried. 'He was perving on Katie.'

Isaac shook his head. 'No, I wasn't.'

'She told me, and Shona.'

'Is this true?' Ruth said.

'I said no, didn't I?' Isaac gasped in surprise. 'Surely you don't believe me over him?'

Ruth said nothing. She grabbed Isaac by the elbow and marched away with a muttered apology in Donna's direction.

Donna glared at Nate. 'You can't go around accusing folk if you—'

'Katie told me, and I believed her. What would you have done?'

'I would have said something in a little less public place.' She sighed. 'I was on my way home. Are you coming?'

'Where's Shona?'

'Already gone back with Jacob.'

Nate nodded, and they turned to leave. All eyes were still on them, but for once, Donna refused the urge to shout out, too. She wanted to get back to the safety of their home and grieve in peace.

CHAPTER THIRTY-TWO

When the crowds had thinned out completely, Allie gathered the team, and they set off back to the police station. Perry, beside her on the passenger seat, yawned loudly.

'Keeping you up, are we?' Allie teased, then yawned herself.

They grinned at each other.

'It's okay for you. I'll have to prep for the press conference in the morning. Weekends weren't always made for dancing,' Allie chided. 'But I for one can't wait to see my bed this evening. I am bushed.'

'Old.' Perry chuckled. 'Old not bushed.'

'Cheeky git.' Allie punched him in the arm, steadying the steering wheel with one hand for a second. 'And there was me going to call at the chippy on the way back.'

'Fish supper for me.' Sam sat forward. 'It's definitely my shout.'

Once food was grabbed and they were seated at their desks, they set about catching up on what they'd seen or heard that evening. Sadly, Allie weighed up that there wasn't much to go on. It would have been better to have a lead by close of day, but most of the time that came when forensics were in. Speaking of which, she updated the team on an email she'd had from Dave Barnett.

'There's only traces of Katie's blood so far,' she said with a sigh. 'No fibres or hairs et cetera on the body or clothes. Katie's phone and bag are still missing, which is a damn shame. Hopefully we'll have more to go on tomorrow.'

'But the phone is still switched on?'

'As far as we know, but not active. It's been triangulated within half a mile of where Katie was found, so the search team are still looking for it. There are so many houses in that vicinity that it would take an age to get warrants for them all, but that may be something for a later date. However, that will also depend on battery life dying over time.'

'Man, that was good.' Perry wiped his hands on a cleansing wipe once he'd finished his meal and then pointed to his bloated stomach. 'Buddha belly!'

Allie, who'd been reading an email from her phone, glanced up. 'I think you can take that belly home now. Jenny says she doesn't need me until the morning, so we won't have to man the phones as first thought.' She stood up and walked towards her office. 'All of you, let's call it a night.'

With sighs of relief and quiet chatter, Perry, Sam, and Frankie began to tidy up and gather their things. It was half past nine; they'd been working fourteen hours flat. Time for them all to get some rest as tomorrow would be more of the same.

Once alone, Allie took a breather as she sat in the quiet for a moment. After the hustle and bustle of the day, it felt quite decadent. It also gave her time to think. There were so many unanswered questions, and she made a mental list of what to do first thing in the morning. She'd also catch up with what came in overnight, and perhaps there would be more forensic results from Dave.

It only took one mistake to catch a killer. And Allie and her team were all over it.

CHAPTER THIRTY-THREE

Three months ago

Katie stretched out in Ethan's bed. He'd gone to make breakfast and coffee. They hadn't got in until late after a Saturday night out in Flynn's, and Katie had been so tired she hadn't even sneaked in with Ethan as planned. Now his parents were out shopping, she'd rushed along the landing to jump on him.

She grinned, unable to believe how her status had risen since they'd become an item. It had been a game-changer going out with Ethan, and she liked it a lot. Girls who'd never speak to her before noticed her now, in awe when Ethan was holding her hand.

She decided to take a quick shower, so she'd be all fresh and clean for when he came back to bed. The warm water hitting her body relaxed her, and she smiled with satisfaction as she enjoyed its warmth.

She heard something close and, expecting to see Ethan,

turned to give him a full view of her nakedness. But it wasn't him.

Isaac had come into the room.

'Get out!' she cried, covering herself up as much as she could.

Isaac looked her up and down in a leery manner. 'Very nice.'

Katie reached for the towel, but Isaac pulled it away from her.

'Give it to me,' she snapped.

He stood there laughing.

'Ethan!' she shouted.

Isaac threw the towel onto the floor of the shower. It landed in a puddle of water.

'I could take you any time I like,' he sneered.

'You wouldn't even get first dibs,' she replied. Really, she wanted him to leave so that she could stoop to get the towel.

But Isaac stepped forward and cupped a hand to her breast.

She tried to move it, but he squeezed hard. She kept her face straight, so as not to give him any satisfaction, but inside she was furious. And a little scared.

'What's Ethan's is mine,' Isaac told her. 'We've always shared as brothers.'

Katie knew the best thing she could do was not show how much he was scaring her. She smiled, reaching down for him. Then she grabbed his crotch and squeezed as hard as he had done to her. As his face contorted, she firmed her grip.

'You're a snake for doing this on your brother, but I don't suppose it'll be the first time.'

'Let me go, you bitch,' he seethed.

'Come near me again when I'm vulnerable and I'll let everyone know what a sexual predator you are quicker than you can say my dick is so tiny. Do you hear?'

'You all right, babe?' Ethan shouted up the stairs. 'Did you want me for something?'

'No, I'm good thanks. Just need coffee!' Katie held on to Isaac for a moment longer and then released him. She picked up her towel and covered herself. 'Now, get out of here before I really do scream.'

Isaac glared at her before leaving the room. His eyes were the darkest she'd seen them, and she was certain she hadn't heard the last of it but, even though she was shaking, she'd had to show him who was boss.

She dried herself quickly, dressed in one of Ethan's T-shirts, and got back into bed. She wasn't sure if she should say anything to Ethan or not, because it would probably start a fight. So when he came into the room, with a tray of hot drinks and toast, she smiled as if nothing had happened.

They shared breakfast, and then Ethan drew back the duvet.

'Where are you off to?' she asked.

'I've got to go soon, so I'm going to take a shower.'

Katie pulled him towards her.

'Hey.' Ethan protested, but it was short-lived as she kissed him. Right now, she needed reassurance that she was his and his alone.

CHAPTER THIRTY-FOUR

Tommy Mason missed his footing as he came out of The Fox and Hare and nearly ended up going arse over tit. Luckily, there was a lamppost in front of him by the side of a hedge, which slowed his momentum. He wrapped his arms around it, coming to a stop then, laughing to himself, straightened out his jacket before going again.

It had been a skinful kind of evening. After Katie's vigil earlier, most of the neighbours and people who knew her had congregated in the pub. It had been a sad event that had turned into a high-spirited knees-up. Well, not so many knees, but a lot of drowning sorrows.

Tommy had known Katie since forever as he'd hung around with Nate and they'd all gone to the same school. He'd always liked her, even as the baby of the family, and had felt protective of her. Sure, they'd had their arguments as they'd grown up around one another, but he'd always looked out for her.

Having said that, last month the barney they'd had was enormous. Tommy hadn't seen much of her since then, and he wondered now if it was going to be his downfall.

Katie had told him a few home truths about Ethan and his brother. She'd needed to get it off her chest. Of course he wasn't going to say anything to anyone about it, especially the police. He didn't want the wrath of Ethan or Isaac Riley, never mind the prick they worked for on the side.

All he'd wanted to do at the party on Friday was see if she was okay. He hoped it hadn't got her into grief and someone had taken it out on her.

Tommy sauntered down the street, wobbling about but managing to stay upright. He was going to be wasted tomorrow morning. He hoped he wouldn't sleep through his alarm.

'Oi, Mason, we want a word with you.'

Tommy turned round to see who was addressing him. He squinted, peering in the dark, but he couldn't make out who it was. Until two faces revealed themselves as they passed under the lamppost. His shoulders dropped.

'What's up, lads?' he said, spying the Riley brothers.

'You know more about Katie than you're letting on,' Ethan said.

Tommy shook his head, seeing double but still trying to stay focussed. 'Don't know what you mean.'

'You were trying to get her to yourself at the party.'

'I never did anything!' A punch in the nose came first. His head reared backwards, and he staggered to the right.

'She was dropped off near to home. There are only so many lunatics and weirdos who live in the avenue, and you're one of them.'

Tommy didn't like that they were making fun of him, but he knew when his luck had run out.

'You hurt her and you're going to pay, weirdo,' Isaac joined in.

A fist flew at him, and then another from the opposite

direction. Tommy hadn't had many fights, and even then, it had been one on one when he'd been sober.

He put up his hands to fend off the brothers, but the punches rained down on him. He dropped to the ground and curled in a ball, hoping they would do what they had to do and move on. But the kick to the head rendered him useless to defend himself. He blacked out after the second one.

MONDAY - DAY THREE

CHAPTER THIRTY-FIVE

Perry groaned as the alarm went off in his ear. Blindly, he reached out with a hand and found the snooze button. 'It can't be morning yet.'

'You have to get up,' Lisa mumbled.

'It's dark.'

'I know.'

He turned towards her and spooned into her back. 'A few more minutes.'

They lay together in the dark. Perry sighed, content but annoyed that he had to make a move. It wasn't fair on Lisa to listen to the alarm going off again.

A minute later, he drew back the duvet and sat on the edge of the bed. He reached for his phone, slid back the alert button, and stretched his arms above his head.

It was ten past six. Perry enjoyed his job, but if there hadn't been a murder, he wouldn't be due at the station until eight. Swings and roundabouts. A shower, followed by a mug of strong coffee, was what he needed.

Downstairs fifteen minutes later, coffee was cooling while he ate toast. He didn't normally eat this early as a rule, but he was starving and unsure when he'd next get a break. Murder cases were mostly long days and evenings, sometimes working well into the night, and even stopping for fast food was often sporadic. Before he left, he popped a couple of chocolate bars in his coat pocket.

He opened the front door and stopped dead in his tracks. On the welcome mat was a small jerry can. By its side was a piece of paper folded in half and a lighter. Perry glanced around the small cul-de-sac. There were only a couple of lights on, and no one around that he could see.

He stooped in front of the can and gave it the once-over. Then he went back into the kitchen, pulled out a pair of latex gloves from a box under the sink, and a bin liner. At the same time, he rang Allie.

'Perry, what's up?'

'There's been a petrol can, lighter, and a note left on my doorstep.'

'Shit, are you okay?'

'Yeah, I'm fine but I need to shift it before Lisa gets up.'

'What does the note say?'

'I haven't looked yet. I'm going to bag it up and bring it in.'

'Okay, then we'll take it from there. Do you want me to come to you? I was on my way out the door.'

'No, I'll meet you at the station.' He disconnected the call and stooped again, picking up the can to see if it was full or if this was an empty threat.

It was full.

He placed it gently inside the bin liner and transferred it to the boot of his car. He had evidence bags in there, so he popped the lighter in one and the note in another. But not before seeing what was written on it. One word.

BOOM.

There was no time to panic or think of the whys and

wherefores. He needed to get to work and take this away from his family.

As he drove, he thought about what it meant. It was a threat for sure, and personal, too. In the job they did, with the enemies they made along the way, there was always the likelihood that something like this would happen. If he had to think of who it might be, there would be a lengthy list of names, most of them still behind bars. Yet there was one name in particular that always stuck in his throat.

Terry Ryder.

It had to be him who was behind it. But then again, it was over two years since they'd put him away for the second time, so why now if so?

Perry would check the doorbell camera and CCTV when he got to his desk, to see if he could spot anyone on it who he knew. He had both apps on his phone.

Allie was in her office when he got there. Frankie waved when Perry passed their desks. 'Sam's making a brew if you want one.'

'Yeah, cheers.' He said nothing about the bag he was carrying, not even when it caught Frankie's attention, and he frowned.

'Hey,' he said when he got to Allie. 'Shall I close the door?'

'Yes, please.' Allie was wearing latex gloves, the blind already pulled down for privacy. 'Take a seat.'

CHAPTER THIRTY-SIX

Donna had been up since quarter to five. It was now half past seven, and she was already weary. She checked the message that had come in on her phone. This time she replied.

'I'm going to get some fresh air,' she said to Shona who was curled up as much as she could beside her on the settee.

'It's early,' Shona said.

'I know. Thought I'd go while there's not too many people around. I won't be long.' Donna grabbed her keys and phone and headed out.

It was cool, the biting wind of the previous week dissipating but still with a nip in the air. Another grey day. Yesterday, Donna had said she couldn't wait for winter to change to spring, and now she'd do anything to put the clock back.

The area was eerily quiet after the crowds the night before. She'd been pleased to see so many people coming to pay their respects.

She thought back to some of the conversations she'd had, upsetting yet heartwarming. She loved her community for that, each of them looking after their own.

It was only a minute before Donna saw the figure above waiting for her.

'Hey,' Woody said, drawing level.

'Hey.' She walked into his outstretched arms. Before he'd even hugged her, she was sobbing. They stood for a moment while she calmed herself, then set off together along the gravel path.

The darker months were far better for having an affair, she mused, as they went out of view. She'd never meant to start it, but like so many people say, it just happened. One minute they were friends. The next they were kissing, and it led to the inevitable.

At first, she'd been disgusted with herself, and him, but she'd wanted to do it again as soon as they could. She knew in the back of her mind that she was on the rebound, that Max's death was making her miss being part of a couple. She met lots of single men at work, and yet, she chose to steal someone else's husband. And not just any husband. If they were ever found out, the fallout would be unimaginable.

He seemed nervous, maybe because this was the first time they'd been alone together since Katie's death.

'I don't really know what to say,' he said. 'Nothing I can think of will make you feel any better. I am so shocked.'

'I don't want words. I need comfort.'

He pulled her near. 'I think we'll have to be extra careful for a while.'

'I know.' She sighed loudly. Everything was far more complicated now, yet she did want to see him. She had to get out of the house every now and then, and she also wanted someone to talk to. She had Hannah and Shona, but their arms didn't soothe her as much as his.

'Did you go on okay when you identified Katie?' he asked. 'I can't begin to think how hard that would be. I wish I could have gone with you.'

Donna nodded, choked at the thought of her little girl lying dead in a mortuary. 'Her necklace is missing,' she told him. 'I bought her a heart-shaped locket when she was sixteen, and she's worn it ever since. It wasn't with her. I hope the police find it because a part of my heart will always be with it if they don't.'

'You're sure she was wearing it?'

'She never takes it off.'

'Then the police will find it. What else is happening with the enquiry?' he asked. 'Any updates?'

'There was nothing late last night. It's as if her killer vanished.'

'Oh, love. That's terrible.'

'The family liaison officer will be here at nine, so she'll update me if anything has come in overnight.'

'Will you let me know if there is? Send me a message. I'd like to be there for you, even if it's only over the phone.'

Donna nodded, and they turned back to go home.

'I'm sorry we fell out on Friday,' he said. 'It was silly.'

'It's irrelevant now,' she replied. 'But we do need to think about the future. What's right for our families as well as us.'

'I can't bear to lose you.'

'I know, but what we're doing is immoral. The pain I feel losing Katie makes me realise how wrong.' She didn't say that even though she needed him now, the arrangement they had couldn't go on much longer. She didn't want to be with him. She simply wanted someone to hold, to be with, to feel loved.

She was contradicting herself, because she shouldn't be doing any of that with him. And it didn't matter now because it had to end. Things were too close to home, always had been.

She'd tell him when all this was over. Right now, she didn't have the bandwidth for any more drama.

CHAPTER THIRTY-SEVEN

Perry popped the bags on the desk, and Allie glanced inside each one in turn. When she came to the note, her eyes widened.

'*Are* you okay?'

'Yes and no. This is my family someone is messing with.'

'I'll get this rushed to the lab to see if there are prints on it. My guess will be that there won't, but it's worth a shot.'

'I'm going to check the apps on my phone to see what time it was put there.'

'Yes, then we can get Sam to do a recce around the streets nearby for any vehicles.' She paused. 'I'm going to take this to Jenny, and we'll have to tell the rest of the team.'

He nodded. 'I don't know what to do about Lisa. Should I warn her in case someone follows through with the threat? Or should I say nothing in case the threat is empty? I don't want to worry her.'

'I'd tell Mark if it were me, because I'd need him to be vigilant. Even if that concerned him. I think it's better to be prepared.'

'Perhaps she could go and stay with her mum for a few

days. I know the threats will remain, but the imminent danger might be gone. What I can't understand is its connection to the case we're working on. Do you think this had Terry Ryder's stamp on it?'

Allie shuddered inwardly at the thought. 'There's been nothing yet to suggest he had anything to do with Katie or the Frost family.'

'Unless we haven't found it yet?'

'But why now? It doesn't make sense.' Allie sat back in her chair and blew out a breath. 'Get yourself into the incident room and check over the footage on your phone. Take as much time as you need. I'll pass it over to Sam if necessary.' She then picked up her desk phone. 'I'll contact Jenny, because we'll have to make this official.'

Perry came out of the office and across the floor. Sam wasn't back from tea duties, but Frankie was there.

'Everything okay, Perry?' he asked.

He nodded, then went to the bathroom. He stood in front of the sink, staring at himself in the mirror, hands clasping the worktop. What the fuck was going on? His eyes filled with tears at the thought of someone doing anything to his family. His wife and his boy were his world.

He dried his wet cheeks and, with shoulders held high to show the confidence he wasn't feeling, went back on the floor and walked on to the incident room. Sam gave him a faint smile as he passed by. It was obvious Frankie had warned her something was wrong.

And then he got down to studying the footage from his phone. If it took forever for him to identify the culprit, then so be it. He wasn't leaving until he had at least a few suggestions as to who might be behind it all.

. . .

After hearing what had happened, Sam had thought of nothing else but the photographs which had been left on her car. Once Frankie had nipped downstairs and she could see Perry in the incident room, she took the moment to talk to Allie.

'I didn't say anything immediately because I didn't connect the two things at first,' she said afterwards. 'I thought it might have been someone stirring up trouble, rather than someone out to get me. But also, it's embarrassing admitting it to the team. I don't want anyone to think ill of me.'

'It's not our problem what you do in your free time. We're all here if you want to talk about it, although it will be hard as we all know Craig. But you have to do what's right for you.'

'I've been thinking about leaving him for a while, but it's complicated with Emily and childcare.'

'I get it, Sam. You don't have to explain yourself to any of us.' Allie held up her hand. 'How do you want to play this? Do you want me to keep it to myself and see if anything else happens?'

'No! You can tell them. I'd never forgive myself if my incident turns out to be linked to Perry's.' She paused. 'Can you tell them when I'm not there, though?'

'Sure, no problem.' Allie thought of saying more but stopped short. It wasn't her business, but she did want to say one thing. 'This is not your doing, remember that.'

Allie was on her way back from Jenny's office. The DCI had arranged for officers to patrol the streets around Perry's home for a few nights while the incident was investigated. Allie would have preferred it if Lisa wasn't staying there, and she hoped Perry would talk some sense into her going eventually.

Before the main morning's briefing, she gathered together

her direct team and updated them on what had happened, sending Sam off to make coffee and then come back with red cheeks.

'Does this mean someone will come after me now?' Frankie asked. 'Or you, boss?'

Allie shook her head. 'I have no idea, but I think we all need to be careful, at home and at work. If someone is targeting each of us deliberately, then something could happen at any time. I want you to speak to Lyla and bring her up to speed. You, too, Sam, get in touch with Craig. Perry and I will do the same. Hopefully nothing else will happen, but we can't be sure. In the meantime, we need to see if we can spot who delivered the message.' She glanced at her watch. 'I'll delay full team briefing.'

As they got out their phones, Allie took a moment for herself. It wasn't going to be easy for any of them.

Then she reached for her mobile and called Mark.

CHAPTER THIRTY-EIGHT

At nine-thirty, everyone involved in Operation Meakin piled into the incident room. Allie's team, sitting at the front, were looking a little jaded.

'It's important that we all stay observant,' she told them. 'We now have two cases of officers, or their homes being targeted, so there may be more. Also, keep in regular contact with your loved ones, all of you, okay?' When there were lots of nods, she continued. 'Frankie, want to update us on the details of the party?'

Allie's phone rang halfway through him speaking. She moved away to answer it. 'When was this? Okay, yes, we can go straightaway. I'm almost done with the briefing now.' She disconnected the call with all eyes on her. 'Tommy Mason was beaten up last night. He's in the Royal Stoke. Apparently, he was at the vigil and then in the pub afterwards and someone jumped him when he left.' She glanced around the room. 'Frankie, seeing as you know all about the party, come with me.'

'On it, boss.'

Allie nodded her thanks and addressed the rest of the room. 'Stay safe out there. Remember, be wary of anything that seems out of the ordinary. Call it in first if you're fearful of it being a repercussion.'

Allie and Frankie made their way to the Royal Stoke Hospital. They found Tommy Mason in A&E on a trolley in a long corridor with several other patients. He watched as they came towards him, his face swollen, butterfly stitches above his eye and a large bruise to the side of his face.

Liz Mason was standing by his side when they reached him.

'Oh, now you arrive,' she said, staring directly at Frankie. 'You said there would be a police presence to stop this kind of thing happening.'

'Nan!' Tommy cried. 'Don't be so embarrassing.'

'Embarrassing?' Liz shook her head. 'I've a good mind to leave you to it then, you ungrateful—'

'Please.' Allie held up her hand. 'There are other patients here, too.' She took out her warrant card and introduced herself. 'To get to the bottom of this, we need some details from Tommy.' When she saw Liz was calming down, she addressed him. 'How are you?'

'Sore, but I'll live.' He gave a half-smile, then winced. 'Sorry, I didn't mean anything by that. I have a few injuries but nothing more.'

'They've kept him in because of concussion,' Liz told them. 'He was throwing up until a couple of hours ago.'

'When did you arrive?' Allie moved closer to the trolley, Frankie and Liz doing the same to allow a man in blue scrubs to rush past wheeling a blood pressure monitor.

'Last night,' Liz replied. 'Around half past ten. Someone

coming out of the pub found him not long after it happened. They called me, and I rang a taxi straightaway.'

'Did you see who attacked you, Tommy?'

Tommy shook his head. 'It was dark.'

'You were too drunk more like,' Liz chastised. She rolled her eyes at Frankie and Allie. 'He was in the pub after Katie's vigil, and he had far too much.'

'Was it one person, or two, or a few?' Frankie opened his notebook, pen poised.

'There were two of them, but they were wearing ballys.'

'Did you see what else? Any designer labels on their coats or jackets?'

'No, I saw nothing.'

'You saw nothing?' Liz shook her head in exasperation. 'These people are here to help, and yet you still adhere to a code of loyalty that won't allow you to say anything else?'

'Nan, I didn't see... okay?'

'Will you be quiet along there, or I'll have to ask you to leave?'

'Sorry,' they all said in unison.

'We were told you were at the Bennett Cricket Club, attending Abigail Matthews's party on Friday night,' Allie said, 'and that there was an argument with you and Katie's boyfriend. Can you tell us what happened?'

'There's not much to say. I was talking to Katie when Ethan came barging over. He threatened me, said if I ever looked at Katie again, he'd floor me. We weren't doing anything. I've known her since we were kids. She's like a sister to me.'

'What happened after he threatened you?'

'Him and Katie left.'

'How did Katie seem?'

'She was fuming.' Tommy chuckled. Then his face

dropped. 'She could be a feisty one when rattled. I'm going to miss her. Have you got anyone for it yet?'

Allie ignored his thirst for knowledge. 'Are you sure your attack wasn't linked to that incident?'

'I don't see how when I didn't do anything wrong.'

'But that's not the way Ethan might see it. You're sure it wasn't him and his brother, and you don't want to tell us?'

Tommy glanced away for a moment. 'I'm sure,' he said eventually.

'Then you must have upset someone else. Did they say anything to you, at the vigil perhaps?'

'No, I kept out of their way. And in the pub afterwards, too.'

'So you're certain that the argument at the party and the beating you received weren't linked?'

'Like I said, I don't know.'

Allie knew she wasn't going to get anything useful out of him. Tommy was lying, she was certain. They left them in the corridor and, once outside, she asked Frankie for his thoughts.

'I reckon he knows who it was,' he said. 'He doesn't want to say.'

'I agree. Can you pay him a visit later this afternoon, when he's back at home and might have remembered something he's now willing to share?'

'Will do.'

Allie sighed inwardly. Why did some people think there was always a code of silence to adhere to? If they talked too much, they'd get a beating for being a snitch. But all she wanted to rule out was whether Tommy knew more than he was letting on about Katie – and who gave him such a beating in the first instance.

Her phone rang. She pinched the bridge of her nose while

she listened to the caller. 'We're still at the hospital. We'll check it out.'

'Boss?' Frankie queried.

'There's been a young girl attacked, found in a cut-through off Merchant Road. Hit around the head. We need to find Ward 107.'

CHAPTER THIRTY-NINE

Allie and Frankie sanitised their hands again before going into the ward. They were shown into a waiting room, thankfully empty, while the nurse went to fetch the relatives of seventeen-year-old Chloe Barker.

'Do you think it's too early to think they're connected, boss?' Frankie asked.

'Yes, and no.' Allie sighed. 'I hope we don't have a serial attacker. Maybe his or her intention was to kill Chloe, too, but she survived. We'll find out more when her—'

The door opened, and a man came in. His smile was faint, his face gaunt. He seemed as if he'd had every ounce of life taken from him. In his mid-forties, he was well dressed, facial hair beginning to show a shadow over his chin. He held out a hand when he reached them. 'I'm Mick Barker, Chloe's dad.'

Allie introduced both her and Frankie, and they sat down.

'How is she doing?' Allie asked first.

'She's in a bad way but stable.' He shook his head in disbelief. 'The times I've heard that on the news and not taken any notice of it. You don't expect it to happen to your child.'

'Are you able to tell us what happened? We know the brief details but would like to hear from you, too.'

'It was half past eight, and Mac, our dog, needed to go out for his last walk. Chloe offered to take him, and I-I said it was okay. We don't go far, he's getting on a bit now, so I knew she wouldn't be long.' Mick's hand formed a fist, and he held it in front of his mouth while he composed himself. 'Her mum and I were watching TV, and it wasn't until half an hour had passed that we began to wonder where she was. We thought perhaps she'd taken him for a longer walk, so Diane rang her. We got no answer so we both went out to look for her, tracing the way we'd all go with Mac.'

'Where is that, Mr Barker?' Allie asked, glancing at Frankie to see he had a notepad at the ready.

'We live in Claypot Avenue. His walk is around the block there, takes ten minutes at the most. We checked the route she would have taken but we couldn't find her. It was really bizarre. We tried calling her constantly, but there was no reply.'

'Was the phone ringing out or switched off?'

'It kept ringing. Diane left a message for the first few times we tried. And then we saw someone running along Merchant Road.'

Allie and Frankie sat forward at this.

'Coming towards you or away from you?' Allie wanted to know.

'Towards, passed, and then away from us. We didn't take any notice at first. But then we glanced at each other and ran in the direction he'd come from. I don't know why, but as we drew closer, we could hear Mac barking.' A half sob came from him.

'You're doing great, Mick.' Allie leaned across to place a friendly hand on his arm, giving him a moment to compose himself. She tried to blank all the images that were pushing themselves towards her of her sister. Allie had never seen her until Karen had been at the hospital.

'There was a walkway, one we wouldn't use, so I don't know why she was up there. We shouted Mac, but he wouldn't come to us. He paced up and down whimpering, and that's when we saw her. She was lying on the grass at the side of the gravel path. We called for an ambulance, and the rest you know.'

'I'm sorry you had to go through it all again for us, but as you can imagine, every little detail will help us to find who did this to Chloe. We'll start house-to-house enquiries soon to gather as much information as we can. Can you tell us any more about the person you saw running away? It might not be connected to what happened but at the same time it could be crucial.'

'It was a male, about late teens to early twenties at a guess. He was wearing dark clothes – there was some sort of yellow logo on the back of his hoodie. I couldn't tell you if he had hair or what colour it was because he had a beanie hat on. That was black, too.'

'Did you get a look at his face?'

Mick shook his head. 'For a fraction of a second when he clocked us but not enough to see anything other than he was white.'

'That's really useful,' Allie said, feeling helplessness emanating from him. She raised her eyebrows at Frankie, so he knew she had finished, and stood up.

'We'll keep in touch, Mr Barker.' She handed him a card. 'Take my contact details and call me any time you need to. If there's anything else you think about over the next few hours, do let us know. Sometimes details come back to victims later after the trauma.'

Mike took it from her and nodded his thanks.

Allie and Frankie left the ward with heavy hearts. The

thoughts of what happened to her sister and how her life changed in an instant still haunted Allie. She hoped Chloe would recover and would be the same as she was before. Obviously, she'd be mentally damaged by what had happened, but she prayed she wasn't left in a vegetative state like Karen.

That would be the worst outcome all round.

CHAPTER FORTY

Two months ago

'Hey, dirty stop out,' Shona teased Katie once she got home. 'I haven't seen you in a couple of days. Have you been shacked up with lover boy?'

Katie grinned at her sister as she put down her holdall. 'I might have been, but in between there was college.'

'Has that lech at the shop been behaving himself?'

'Me and Beth quit. He was getting on our nerves.'

Shona was referring to Sebastian who worked at the mini market with Katie. He was quite creepy, especially when he got her alone. He was eight years older than Katie, and the manager's son. But Katie wasn't having any of it, and when she'd told him, he said he was going to let his dad know she was crap at her job.

'Good for you.'

'How are you?' She rested her hand on Shona's stomach.

Shona was five months pregnant now and literally glowing. Katie had never seen her so happy, and she couldn't wait to meet her niece.

'I'm tired but okay.' Shona put her hand over Katie's. 'I can't believe I have a baby growing in there. I mean, how on earth will I get her out?'

'Well,' Katie teased. 'You'll be admitted to a labour ward and—'

'You know what I mean.' Shona flapped away her comment. 'I'm scared of giving birth.'

'Mum had three of us. Imagine.' Katie gave a look of mock horror. 'I suppose it's something women have to go through. I can't wait to have kids in the future but not for a long time yet.'

Shona smiled at her. 'So you're still in love?'

'I am.' Katie beamed. 'Ethan bought me a teddy, can you believe that? I'm not sure if it's romantic or childish, but it's a nice thought.'

'Let me see.'

Katie rummaged in her holdall, pulled out the bear, and passed it to Shona. It was a white fluffy one with red dungarees, and it was holding a heart in its paws.

'Aw, sweet.' Shona frowned. 'What's in its pocket?'

Katie leaned across the table to see what Shona was pointing at. There was a small bulge. 'I hadn't noticed that. Let me see.'

Shona passed it back, and Katie removed a small black object. It was her turn to frown. 'It's a memory stick.'

'Oh! I wonder if he's recorded you a love note. Or a video!'

'Don't be daft. This is Ethan we're talking about. He'd send me something on my phone.'

'But perhaps this is private, maybe more personal.' Shona shuddered. 'I hope it's not a dick pic.'

'I hope it's not a dick pic either!' Katie popped the memory stick into her pocket.

'You're not going to see what it is?'

She shook her head. If it was something Ethan wanted no one else to see, then she wasn't going to open it in front of Shona, sister or no sister. It could be embarrassing.

'Well, you run upstairs and view it and then let me know,' Shona said. 'Because if you don't, I'm going to wonder about it all night.'

'Okay.' Katie grinned and went to her room. She opened her laptop, and while it booted up, she speculated on what it would be. If it was a dick pic, she was going to be so embarrassed. And annoyed.

Maybe he was showing her something he'd done for her. Announcing he'd got tickets to a show or a holiday even. But, again, he'd do that over the phone, surely?

She pushed the memory stick into the port. A folder appeared, titled ISSAC. She clicked on it and found a video. Katie opened it and gasped, her hand covering her mouth. She couldn't believe what she saw. If the police were to see it, Isaac would be in big trouble.

After viewing it several times, she took the stick out and closed the laptop lid.

What was going on? Why would Ethan give that to her? Why would he even keep it in the first place?

Was it a test of loyalty? Did he want her to hide it, or had he left it with her for safekeeping? Either way, he should have asked first. And there was she, thinking it was a romantic gesture.

Katie reached for her phone to call Ethan and then she stopped. *Could* this be a test? Should she tell him about it or keep quiet? She couldn't decide which to do. For now, she put her phone down.

But after a few minutes, she realised the video on the memory stick could be *her* security, too, if anything went wrong. Something to bargain with.

She would keep it for now. Because after seeing what was on the file, she wasn't sure she wanted to be a part of the Riley family anymore, Ethan or no Ethan. That wasn't her scene.

The door to her room opened, and Shona appeared, making Katie jump.

'Well?' her sister asked, clearly excited.

Katie grinned, hoping to fool her. 'It's a soppy thing. I can't show you, it's too personal.'

'Aw, the big softie. I wish Jacob would do something like that for me.'

Katie's smile was wide, but inside she was breaking. Her sister thought Ethan was mad about her. Maybe it was better that way. She yawned loudly, hoping Shona would get the message.

'I'm happy for you, little sis,' Shona said. 'You deserve someone like Ethan if he loves you so much. Night. Sweet dreams.' She blew Katie a kiss.

Once Shona had left, Katie glanced around the room. She needed a hiding place for the stick until she could figure out what to do with it. It had to be somewhere Nate wouldn't find it. She couldn't risk it getting into his hands.

But then, she realised the safest place was probably on her at all times. She reached for her handbag. Inside it was a makeup pouch, with several pockets inside. She popped the stick in one of those, hiding it well within all her paraphernalia. It was as safe a place as any.

With it hidden away, Katie's mind began to settle. The situation wasn't ideal, but until she'd learned more about why Ethan had given the stick to her, it was staying with her there.

CHAPTER FORTY-ONE

The first thing Allie noticed when they got to Redgrave Street was Perry talking to an elderly gentleman. Her DS gave a nod of acknowledgement as she drove past and parked as near to the scene as possible. Crime scene tape was tied across the entry, and several police cars were already on site.

The Major Crimes Team investigated all kinds of things as well as the odd murder, and as this was a serious assault, it would be policed with as much diligence. What Allie really wanted to know was if the attack on Katie and Ella were linked. She hoped not, but it seemed a tad coincidental that two females would be hit around the head, one dead and one possibly left for dead.

Was it the running man who was their suspect for assaulting Ella, or was he an innocent passerby who had run from the scene in a panic, maybe to get some help? Had he been disturbed, she mused, glancing around once out of her car. She wouldn't rule out any possibility right now.

There were several residents from the street standing on their doorsteps and looking out of windows, but no one was crowding the entry. Allie waved at Dave Barnett, who was a few metres away when he caught her eye, and waited while he came towards her.

'That'll be the druggies,' someone from across the street shouted over.

Allie and Frankie turned to see a man in his forties with folded arms resting on a large stomach. 'They're always causing havoc across there. We've asked the council to close it off, but do they ever listen? Shame it'll take something like this to get their attention.'

'Frankie, head over and get some details, will you?' she told him.

'How is the girl doing?' Dave asked when he drew level with her.

'They kept her in because of her head wound, but she's stable.'

'That's great to hear.'

'With any luck someone will have seen something last night. At the very least we have a young guy running away, which will hopefully have been captured on someone's CCTV or Ring camera.'

'Any jewellery found?'

'Not that I'm aware of. You're thinking the case could be linked to Katie Frost?'

'I need the evidence to say yes or no.'

'At your service, ma'am.' Dave doffed an imaginary cap. 'After a little rain during yesterday afternoon, we have some prints in the mud. Size ten, look like a male's boot. Apart from that, there's nothing else to do for me.'

'So I can get the officers searching the immediate area?'

'You can. Give me five to pack up and I'll be on my way.'

'Thanks.' Allie saw Simon and went over to him.

'Nasty stuff,' he said. 'A bit worrying, too. Are the cases connected?'

'We don't know yet.' She smirked. 'That's all I can tell anyone, never mind you.'

'I know, I know. Worth a shot.' Simon pointed along the street. 'I'll hang around here to see if anyone saw anything.'

'Nice article over the weekend. It was handled sensitively. I'm glad you wrote it.'

'Thanks. I do my best.'

'You do! It was lovely to see you and Grace last week, by the way. Thanks for the presents.'

'All down to Grace, but I'll let her know.'

The smile on his face at the mention of his wife's name was lovely to see.

Perry joined them. 'Got some intel coming through from the street,' he said after greeting them both. 'We have two images of a male running and three CCTV cameras that have picked him up.'

'Is his face visible?'

'Not on the two that I've seen as he was moving so fast. But there are more neighbours to talk to. Do you think he's our guy?'

'If he isn't, what was he running from?'

'Or he could have been late for someone. Maybe he didn't see our victim.'

'I suppose she was pretty hidden, but the dog would have been barking. The parents said he wouldn't leave her, not even to come to them when they shouted him.'

'Humans could learn a lot from the loyalty of a dog,' Allie mused. 'But right now, our main priority is to rule Running Man in or out so we can press on. I'd hate to think he was our killer, leaving someone for dead and out there able to do it again. We also need to see if there is any link between Katie and Chloe. Can you call Rachel and get her to ask the family?'

Perry nodded.

Allie, realising Simon was still there, frowned.

Simon held up a hand. 'You know me better than to think I'd use any of what you'd just said.'

'I do, thankfully. Now bog off and get what you can of that in the paper ASAP. And send my love to Grace. Tell her we need a night out, the two of us, and soon.'

'But you only saw her five days ago!'

'And we were with you and Mark, so we couldn't gossip about married life.'

His look was one of absurdity now.

'Kidding.' She chuckled. 'Well, a little bit.'

Perry, who had walked a few feet away to make a phone call, beckoned her over.

'There's a slight connection with Katie and Chloe. They both go to Staffordshire College and are on a business course. They're in the same lectures for a few subjects. But there's been no trouble with either of them, individually or together as far as was known. Katie was friends with Beth Murray, and Chloe with Ashleigh Matthews and Harriet Stanley.'

Allie pouted. *Could* this be about the party? Did someone say something that riled up another person, blowing things out of proportion? Sometimes the smallest of things could start a deadly fight.

But this was females being attacked.

'There's a connection here somewhere,' she said. 'I wonder if it might be worth sending Frankie to have a word with the students in the same lessons as the two girls.'

'Could be,' Perry agreed.

They said their goodbyes, and Allie made her way back to her car. All the while her mind tried to sort out the puzzle. There were far too many pieces that didn't fit right now. But one thing kept coming back to her.

The party.

CHAPTER FORTY-TWO

Allie was in her car when a call came in. Seeing it was an unknown number, she pulled over to the side of the road to take it.

'DI Shenton,' she said.

'Oh, hello. It's Mike Barker, Chloe's father. You said I should tell you if we found anything out?'

'Yes, I did. How is she doing?'

'She has some more bruising appearing on her neck, at the front. We noticed that her necklace isn't within her personal belongings, and we wondered if it had been broken in the attack.'

'It's possible. I can ask the search team to look around the streets nearby, but nothing was found at the crime scene.' Allie rested the phone on her shoulder while she reached for her notepad. 'What is it like?'

'Gold belcher chain with the letter C on a pendant. It was twenty inches long. I know because I fetched it from the jeweller's. It was her Christmas present last year. She barely ever takes it off.'

'Well, I'll give you a call back once I've spoken to the

team. Is there anything else you can think of, or know is missing?'

'No, nothing. I hope you can find it, but I'll happily buy her a new one. When would you like to speak to her?'

'Right now, if possible. I know it feels intrusive but—'

'We'll do anything we can to catch the bastard who did this to our daughter,' he butted in.

Mr Barker's voice broke with emotion, so Allie ended the call. She put another one through to Sam for her to chase up the search team. Because if that necklace was missing, along with the one belonging to Katie Frost, was that the connection they were after? Was someone keeping mementoes from the women attacked? She shuddered at the thought.

It took only minutes before Sam got back to her.

'There was nothing found by the search team, boss,' she said. 'They've been through the streets either side of it.'

'Okay, thanks. That was what I was expecting but nevertheless didn't want to hear.' Allie paused for thought. 'I'll ask Jenny if we can mention it on the next press update. But for now, I'm going with Chloe and Katie being attacked by the same person and it's very much looking like this was a young white male.'

CHAPTER FORTY-THREE

Even though she'd not long come from the hospital, Allie didn't mind going back again. She was pleased to hear Chloe Barker was out of danger. Chloe would take a while to recover, but she was going to be fine.

She found her in a bay of six beds, the second one on the left. Chloe was sitting up in bed, her blonde hair fanned out across the pillow. She seemed pale underneath the bruising, like a little doll.

'Hi, Chloe, I'm Detective Inspector Shenton, Allie. How are you feeling today?'

'Like I've been hit by a train. I want to go home. The doctor says I should be able to tomorrow.'

'I've spoken to your dad twice. Your parents are worried sick. Can you tell me what happened, are you okay to go through it again?'

Chloe grimaced, her swollen eyes brimming with tears. 'They're going to freak out once they find out what I've been doing.'

'Who are?' Allie sat down at the side of the bed.

'My parents. I'd been going out with Isaac Riley for a few

months. At first, he was nice and a good laugh. I thought we were getting on well, but then he asked me to come with him to deliver something. He said we'd be going by train.'

'Did he say what he was taking?'

'Not straightaway.'

'Where did you go?'

'Manchester. He met someone in a pub behind Piccadilly Station. We had a drink and a quick bite to eat. They swapped bags, and then we got the train back to Stoke.'

'How long were you there?'

'About an hour and a half, but the man was only with us for a few minutes.'

'When was this?'

'About four months ago.'

It was a start, but Allie knew there was no point in looking for CCTV that far back. She let Chloe continue.

'When he dropped me off at home, he gave me one hundred pounds and said I could earn more if I did the runs on my own. I asked him what was in the bag, and he said it was best I didn't know.'

'So you started doing runs for him?'

She nodded. 'He can be very persuasive. And he kept dating me, so I thought… I thought he liked me. But I know now he was using me. I did one run on my own, to the same place, and I met with the same man, and I was honestly petrified. I kept waiting for someone's hand on my shoulder as I got back on the train. I thought I was taking over some money, but I didn't realise I was collecting, too. When I checked inside the bag, I nearly died. It was drugs.'

While Chloe poured a glass of water, Allie closed her eyes momentarily. The times she'd been here before. She wished she could get through to youngsters like Chloe just how horrific it would be to get caught and sent to prison. But no doubt, Chloe will have been told the usual 'first time caught might only get you a caution' tale. It was purely that, a story. Each case and sentence very much depended on the number of drugs being carried.

'Go on,' she told Chloe, once she was ready to speak again.

'When I got back to Stoke, Isaac was waiting for me. We drove away and when he dropped me off at home, he gave me one hundred pounds, like he'd said he would. At the time I thought it was easy money, but after three trips to Manchester, I told him I wasn't going to do it again, that it scared me, and I didn't want to get caught. Well, he flipped. He said he had evidence of me doing the work, photos and film on his phone that would put me inside if I didn't do what I was told. He said no one ever stops until he says so. He said I needed to earn my keep.' Tears slid down her cheeks, and she wiped at them, but more followed.

'You're doing well, Chloe,' Allie encouraged.

'He said he didn't think anything of me, that he saw me as collateral, but if I didn't do what he said, then he would show the video to the police and my family. Then he would come after my brother to take my place. I was so scared that I nearly told my mum and dad, but I couldn't. Then he started calling me and messaging me, and when I blocked him, he kept following me in his car. And then when I took our dog for a walk, he was waiting for me. I don't know how he knew I'd be there but—'

'So you're saying it was Isaac Riley who attacked you?'

CHAPTER FORTY-FOUR

Chloe nodded to Allie. 'Isaac started threatening me to keep my mouth shut.'

'About what?'

Chloe didn't say. 'I... I walked off, and that's when he pushed me in the back. I fell, and before I knew it, he was straddling me and... I thought he was going to rape me. But instead he hit out at me. I was scared to tell anyone because he'd threatened me with all sorts. He said I knew too much, and I do.'

'Is this the first time Isaac has attacked you?' Allie's voice was softer now.

'No. He gave me a right beating two months ago. I was in the boxing gym, and he didn't like me being in my shorts and vest in front of people he knew. He told me to cover up. I put on my hoodie, but later when I was leaving, he was waiting for me in the car park. He said I was showing him up and he wouldn't tolerate it. And then he punched me in the face and stomach. He pulled me by my hair over to his car, but I refused to get in.'

'Did anyone see what was happening? Or come to help?'

'There was no one around. But someone drove onto the car park, and it made Isaac stop, so I pushed him away and ran back inside.' Chloe had tears in her eyes again. 'I told my dad I'd been hit too hard at the gym when I was sparring. He was going to ring and complain, but I managed to convince him it was my own fault.'

'So no one else knew about that incident?'

'No, I don't think so. But I can't live my life like this now he's attacked me again, and I'm scared he'll get to Stephen, that's my brother. Can you help me to get away from him?'

Allie wished she could safeguard every woman who came to her with these kinds of problems, but she couldn't.

'I'll need you to make a formal statement, Chloe. It's going to be extremely helpful. But I can't protect you, you do know that?'

Chloe shook her head. 'You have to.'

'I can arrest Isaac for assault and look into it for you. There may be more evidence that comes in after we've spoken to him, plus we can photograph and catalogue your injuries. But I hate to be harsh, unless we can find enough to place Isaac at the scene, it could be your word against his.'

Chloe's bottom lip trembled.

'And what you've told me that you've been doing with him,' Allie added, 'if it's true we can try to prosecute, but the Crime Prosecution Service might not think there is a strong enough case. I need to warn you that if you want to press charges, then it may get rough for you, and I don't know how to stop anyone coming after you. I'm sorry.'

'I don't care. I've had enough. Let him do his worst.'

Allie stopped then. She was about to leave when she remembered she needed to ask Chloe something.

'Did you know Katie Frost well? I know you were doing the same course at college.'

'Yes, she was nice. We shared a few drinks together at Flynn's when Ethan and Isaac were working, too.'

'Were you at the party on Friday, at the Bennett Cricket Club?'

Chloe nodded.

'Did you see anything you think I should know about?'

'No, I don't think so.'

'Okay, if you do remember something, you can always call me. Your dad has my details.' She smiled and then stood up. 'You've been very brave telling me all this. I will need you to make that statement for us?'

'Okay! I'll do it for Katie, if it helps.'

'Thank you. It will help you, too. Believe me, I will do everything in my power to get the person who did this to you.'

CHAPTER FORTY-FIVE

During yesterday's team brief, Allie learned that Sam had been on to the transport police to see if there had been any sightings of Katie Frost on the trains lately, or any tickets bought by her. Frankie had also been tasked with getting information from Flynn's nightclub to see if she'd been there the weekend before her death. With the possibility of a connection, Allie thought she might have to speak to Steve Kennedy at his boxing club, too.

So far only Sam had been successful, with ticket information showing Katie caught a train at least once a week, and there were several bits of CCTV footage where she was alone when travelling to and from Stoke Station.

Frankie, however, had been getting the runaround and hadn't managed to speak to anyone. Perry decided to join him on a visit, despite the weather blowing a hoolie. They caught up with work while they walked from the station to the nightclub, which was on the outskirts of Hanley.

'How's Lisa?' Frankie asked.

'Gone to stay with her mum for a few days, thankfully.' Perry smirked. 'Although she took some persuading. I feel better with her there, though, yet I know something awful could happen at any time, so she and Alfie can't stay away forever.'

'Yeah, Isla is more annoyed than wary. It's the one thing I don't like about this job. Always having to look over your shoulder, or having threats made against you or your family.'

'It's a worry, for sure.'

'I've tried three times to get into Flynn's,' Frankie added as they waited to cross the road at the bottom of Piccadilly. 'And who's to bet that you knock on the door and get right in on the first attempt?'

'Sod's law, Frankie lad.' Perry chuckled. 'It doesn't always happen that way, though. I've been lucky on occasions and hindered on others. It depends on how much they want to hide, or in some instances how much they want us to know that will get someone else in trouble.'

'I can't believe Steve Kennedy bought the club from Terry Ryder.'

Perry snorted. The Kennedys and the Ryders of this world did what they wanted in the hope they weren't ever caught, and even then, they were proud to do time. Sometimes it felt as if the police had no more control over them than a bitch with several puppies running riot.

Terry Ryder had been the bane of their team's life until they'd put him inside for the murder of his wife. When Ryder was re-arrested the minute he stepped out of prison, it had given everyone the greatest of pleasure when he was charged with further crimes.

How Steve Kennedy now owned Flynn's nightclub wasn't so much a mystery but more of a curiosity. Was it to rub Ryder's nose in things, now that his empire was gone? Or was it that he wanted everyone to know that he was the new king on the block?

It had surprised Perry to find out Steve was up to his old

ways as soon as he came out of prison, too. After such a long stretch, Perry would have expected him to retire on the money he'd made beforehand.

But Perry also knew that his wife, Denise, was a shrewd businesswoman and would be keeping an eye on that side of things for him – legal and illegal.

Denise was respectable, Perry would give her that. She and him never saw eye to eye, but they were both hellbent on looking after their families. And Perry's family included his work colleagues as well as Lisa and Alfie.

They reached the nightclub and went past the main entrance and around to the side of the building. A hard knock on a steel door, a tinny voice through an intercom, a buzz, and they were in. Perry took a moment to grin at Frankie who rolled his eyes in jest.

'They knew we'd turn up eventually,' he mused.

Inside, they walked along a dimly lit corridor, the entrance behind them often used to swiftly turf out the riff-raff who were making a nuisance of themselves. The door ahead opened to reveal the nightclub. They stepped inside, almost onto the dance floor.

'It's so weird seeing it in the daytime,' Frankie said, his eyes flitting around.

'You ever come here before you were a cop?'

'Before it was Flynn's, yeah. It was one of those places where you couldn't stand still for too long or else your feet would stick to the floor. Dingy, loud music, even louder friends. Great fun. Happy memories.'

Perry laughed, knowing exactly what he meant.

There was a bar running along the length of the far wall, the person who had most likely let them in, perched on a stool at the end of it. He was drinking a coffee and waiting for them to spot him.

CHAPTER FORTY-SIX

Perry nudged Frankie, and they walked over to the man. There was no stickiness on the floor now. The club itself had been tidied up in more ways than its decor. Its clientele was far less shady, and yet everyone knew it was the place to get a hit if you needed one, a top-up for the night.

'Isaac, good of you to let us in,' Perry said as they drew near. 'I didn't realise you were working here as well as for your father.'

'I'm not working here. I have a few days off so called in to see someone.'

'Great, because while you wait, we're here to collect some CCTV footage.' He sighed. 'I wish this place would move with the times and get a digital system fitted, but that would mean we'd be able to see too much, and quickly, wouldn't it?'

'Don't know what you're talking about.'

'How's Ethan?' Frankie asked.

'Devastated. He really thought a lot of Katie.'

'What about you? Did you get on with her?'

'We had our moments as she could be a right gobby cow, but yeah, she was all right.'

Allie had rung Perry after she'd interviewed Chloe Barker. He kept all thoughts of that under wraps for now. If he told Isaac what they wanted to find out from him, he would clam up about everything else.

'We wondered if there was anything you can tell us about Katie being at the club. Was she a frequent visitor, do you know?'

'Only since going out with Ethan. She wasn't a regular before that. I'd see her the odd weekend but nothing more. They got together one night here, though, and that was that. But I'm not sure if it would have been anything more as Ethan told me she was okay until something better came along.'

Perry stiffened at the lad's nonchalant attitude towards Katie Frost. It was as if he thought nothing of dumping a woman if she didn't match up to his expectations.

'We're after the footage for last weekend,' he said.

Isaac shook his head. 'I think it's wiped every seven days, on a roll, so if she was here the Saturday before, then it would have gone.'

'No worries. We'll take what we can for now.'

'I've told you, she won't be on it.'

'We'll be sure to view it all closely to make sure.' Perry stood his ground.

'I'll have to check first.'

'No need.' Perry took out a search warrant and handed it to him. 'This is only for the equipment used. I can get something for every room if Steve prefers. Is he in?'

Isaac was still looking cocky until he glanced at the paper. Then he shouted. 'Steve!'

A man in his forties popped his head around a door.

'Police need some info. CCTV for the last week.'

'Is this to do with that murdered girl?'

Perry nodded. 'Anything you can give us may help with our enquiries.'

Steve stood still for a moment. Perry knew the staring was in the hope of intimidating them. Keeping them guessing on whether he was going to cooperate or not. In the end, the man nodded.

'I'll get it for you.'

'Anything else?' Isaac got to his feet suddenly, as if he was bored with everything.

'That's all we need to know from the club,' Perry explained. 'But now we have you here, there's something else you can help us with. Isaac Riley, I'm arresting you on suspicion of assault.' He read him the rest of his rights.

'What?' Isaac frowned.

Steve turned back. 'What's going on?'

'There was a vicious attack on a young female last night,' Frankie told him. 'Isaac is helping with enquiries.'

'No, I'm not.' Isaac struggled, pulling his free arm away.

He tried to lash out, but Frankie had already clicked a handcuff around his wrist.

Frankie noticed the marks on his knuckles. 'That's some nasty bruising there. Anyone would think you'd been in a fight.'

Before Isaac could protest, he grabbed his other hand, and Frankie popped the cuff into place on that one, too. He called for a car to collect their prisoner while they waited for Steve to return with the CCTV footage.

Steve's face was like thunder when he reappeared a few minutes later. He handed Perry a CD.

'Ta very much.' Perry smiled. 'We'll be on our way now. Nice to kill two birds with one stone, though.'

The glare Steve threw them had Perry laughing inwardly. Sometimes his job was fun. Especially when it came to scrotes like Isaac Riley and Steve Kennedy.

CHAPTER FORTY-SEVEN

At lunchtime, Allie joined Jenny for the press update. It was the third day of the investigation, and journalists would be after their blood as they hadn't got anyone in custody in connection with it. But they needed their help, too.

Before they addressed the media, Allie updated Jenny with details of what had happened to Chloe Barker.

Jenny pinched the bridge of her nose. 'No matter what we say, everyone is going to think the two cases are linked.'

'They might be, ma'am. It's too early to tell.'

'Well, there should be a way to use that to our advantage if I mention it rather than ignore it. Changing the subject slightly, have you brought Isaac Riley in?'

'Perry and Frankie are out as we speak. I'm ready to interview him straight after this if they pick him up.'

'Okay, let's get this done.' With shoulders up and head high, Jenny moved forwards.

Allie followed her into the press room and to the front table. She pulled out a chair and faced the mob. Behind were two banners advertising Staffordshire Police with relevant telephone numbers and emails for people to contact.

'We're here to give you an update on the murder of seventeen-year-old Katie Frost,' Jenny began. 'Our forensic team and all officers allocated to this case are working around the clock to gather as much information as we can.'

'Do you have anyone in custody yet?' a male voice interrupted.

Allie stared at Will Lawrence who had asked the question, wondering how Jenny would react. But Jenny kept her eyes on the crowd and ignored him. Allie admired how she could do that, because she just wanted to tell the ignorant git to sit down and shut his mouth.

Jenny then went on to give details about the attack on Chloe Barker. There were murmurs around the room as the inevitable cogs started turning.

'We are eager to show people photo and video footage of a white male running from the scene of the crime. He's around five foot ten, slim build, and wearing a black hoodie, dark jeans, and a black cap.'

Allie held the photo stills in each hand while the video was played on a monitor at their side. It was over in seconds but played several times on a loop. The image was grainy; at the best it might be Isaac Riley. So anyone else mentioning names would be good. Jenny knew how to play the long game, too.

'There are also footprints, men's size tens, in the mud alongside our second victim. She too lost a necklace during the brutal attack. At the moment, we are after connections to see if the cases are linked or if we are dealing with two different suspects.

'We are asking the public to be on the lookout for a necklace similar to this one.' Jenny held up a photo of Chloe's neck area with the necklace clearly on view. 'If you know of its whereabouts, or indeed you found it, please contact us on the number on your screen right now or on the local crime hotline. We want to reunite it with its owner.'

'Does it seem like we have a serial killer?' Will Lawrence shouted out. 'Someone who left both women for dead?'

Jenny cleared her throat while trying to keep her face mutual. Allie knew she would be livid at his lack of empathy.

'Please have some respect for the families of the two women,' she replied. 'One has lost their life, and the other is currently in hospital. When we have details to share, you will be the first to know. I won't be taking any further questions.' Jenny stood up and marched out of the room.

Allie followed closely behind to see her pacing the corridor. She'd expected to take questions from the press, so something must have rattled Jenny.

'That idiot is not to come into any more conferences,' Jenny told her. 'You have my authority to turf him out.'

'Thank you, ma'am. It will be my absolute pleasure.'

'The man hasn't got an ounce of compassion, never mind tact.' Jenny spotted him over Allie's shoulder and marched down the corridor.

'You.' She prodded him in the chest. 'You are barred from any further news conferences. Your manner and attitude are appalling.'

'But how will the readers get the news? You're wanting them to bring in a necklace if they find it. How will they know?'

'Firstly, there are other ways for us to share that kind of information. And secondly, Mr Lawrence, I'm sure there will be another journalist from the *Staffordshire News* who could come in your place.'

'I'm sorry, okay!' Will cried.

Jenny was already halfway along the corridor, a hand lifted to indicate she wasn't listening.

Allie couldn't help but smirk as Will was left standing. He

caught her eye, and she shrugged. She wasn't going to put in a word for him, but she also knew that Jenny wouldn't ban him once she'd calmed down. Sometimes things did get to her DCI – and she couldn't blame her for not keeping her cool every now and then. Especially with weirdo Will Lawrence.

Seeing Simon, who seemed to be waiting to speak to her, she gave him the universal sign to call her. He shook his head to indicate there was nothing important and went on his way.

A message had come in on her phone while she had been in the conference.

Got into Flynn's and Isaac Riley was there. We're downstairs booking him into custody.

Allie walked along the corridor in the opposite direction to the press who were spilling out of the room, sad that she didn't have time to catch up with Simon. Out of all the people she dealt with in her day-to-day life, he was one of a handful who she trusted with anything.

But right now, she wanted to have a chat with Isaac.

CHAPTER FORTY-EIGHT

Isaac Riley had refused legal aid, which put Allie on alert. Either he didn't think he needed it or he thought he'd get away with whatever he'd done.

Now she sat opposite him in interview room four. Frankie was next to her, ready to take notes. He opened his laptop and set the machine to record while Allie went through the necessary wording.

Allie smiled at Isaac, ignoring the folded arms and petulant glare he was giving her.

'Isaac, can you tell me about your whereabouts on Sunday evening? I recall seeing you at the vigil around seven, so if you can go from there, please.'

'I was with my brother and a couple of mates. We joined everyone else in the pub.'

'What time did you leave?'

'About half ten.'

'Were you alone or with your brother or said mates?'

'I was with Ethan.'

'So he can vouch for you?'

'Yeah. We both left at the same time.'

'In separate vehicles?'

'No, we were in Ethan's.'

Allie made a note to check that out, first with any cameras and secondly with Ethan if necessary.

'I'm going to show you some footage now. I want you to see if you recognise anyone on it.'

Frankie pressed play. A grainy figure could be seen running along a road.

'Is this you, Isaac?'

'No comment.'

'What's that logo on the back? It's something in yellow, isn't it?'

'I can't tell.'

'It looks as if it could be from Kennedy's Boxing Club.'

Frankie slid a photo of the image across the desk.

'Do you think I'm right, Isaac?' Allie asked. 'Do you recognise it?'

'I said I can't tell.'

'You're a member there, aren't you?'

'Yeah, so?'

Isaac wasn't showing signs of agitation yet, but Allie knew he would when she showed him their next piece of evidence.

She produced a saved file on the computer. It was an image of Isaac with Chloe Barker. They were clearly an item.

'Is that you on the image?' she asked.

Isaac groaned.

'I'm sorry, I didn't get that.'

'Yes, you know it's me.'

'So you admit to having a relationship with Chloe?'

'Don't know her that well.'

'Really? You seem pretty close on photos taken by her and stored on her phone.'

Isaac was quiet for a moment. 'We're not together anymore.'

'Indeed.'

'What's that supposed to mean?'

'We have data from Chloe's phone. Some of the messages sent from you are quite accusatory and threatening, wouldn't you agree?' She read some of them out. '"If you don't keep your mouth shut, you're dead." "I'm going to let everyone know what you've been doing." What do these messages refer to, Isaac?'

'Can't remember.'

'"I'm warning you, once you're in, you can't get out." What does that signify to you?'

'Hey, whatever it is I'm supposed to have done, you have the wrong person. I didn't assault her.'

'We've also located photographic evidence of injuries over her torso. Horrific bruising. She must have been in a lot of pain. What can you tell me about that?'

Isaac folded his arms. 'You said I could stop at any time and get legal advice?'

'Yes, I did.'

'Then I want to do that before I say anything else.'

When Allie and Frankie left Isaac with a custody officer to return him to his cell, Frankie congratulated her on keeping her cool.

'I wanted to lean across and knock some sense into him,' he joked. 'He's so arrogant. I hope you're going to let him stew while we wait for the duty solicitor.'

'Oh, I'll do that, all right. But he's asking for Charles Dinnen. That'll be fun!'

Charles Dinnen and Allie had met on several occasions when interviewing anyone from the Ryder family, and their associates. For him to represent someone else like Isaac Riley was a further blot on his copybook in her eyes.

'Let's not ask him about Friday evening yet,' she said. 'Something went on at that party. We need to look into more details about where all the boys were at the time Katie was murdered first. Fortunately for them, they might have alibis if they are together. Unfortunately for us, though. This might all go down to timing. It will be crucial.' A message came in on her phone. 'Can I leave this with you for now? There's someone who wants to see me. I'll update you later.'

CHAPTER FORTY-NINE

Two weeks ago

Katie waved at Beth when she spotted her coming into the café. They hadn't seen each other in a week, which was unusual to say the least. Katie knew she'd been a bit lax with sending and replying to messages, too. But she was having fun with Ethan and wanted to spend more time with him.

'Hiya. I got your usual.' She smiled and pointed to a large cappuccino.

'Thanks.' Beth sat down across from her.

The café was almost full, lots of kids in school uniforms, a few people on their own dotted here and there taking all the tables. Katie had managed to grab a small one, sitting close to an elderly couple. It wasn't very private so she would have to be careful what she said.

Beth smiled back, but it wasn't her usual bubbly one.

'What's wrong?' Katie wanted to know. 'Are your olds giving you grief?'

'I'm okay.'

'No, you're not.'

'It's... I miss you. I haven't seen you in ages.'

'It's only a week.'

'You know what I mean.'

'I've been out with Ethan.'

'Where to? Manchester? Birmingham? London?' Beth almost sounded envious.

'London *and* Manchester.' Katie beamed, recalling the trips. If it wasn't for the fetching and carrying, she would have enjoyed every minute of both. 'We stayed over in London. It was amazing. We had a gorgeous room. I've never stayed in anything so grand. It cost a fortune, but Ethan—'

'What did you have to do to earn that?' Beth folded her arms.

'I'm not a prostitute.' Katie snapped, a little put out by her insinuation.

'I didn't mean that.' Beth leaned forward. 'But you are carrying something for him.'

Katie tapped her nose twice. 'It's none of your business.'

Beth gave out a huge sigh. 'What happened to us, Katie? We used to share everything, and I feel like I hardly know you anymore.'

'We've grown up, I suppose. It was going to happen at some point.'

'But Ethan Riley? You can do better than him.'

'Why would you say that?' Katie glared at her friend. 'Are you jealous?'

'No!' Beth glanced around before speaking again. Even then she lowered her voice. 'I worry about you, that's all. He's known for using girls and dumping them, and I don't want you to get hurt.'

'He won't dump me. He loves me.'

Beth's eyes widened in disbelief. 'Are you really that stupid? He's using you as his mule.'

'He is not!' Katie paused, then sneered at Beth. 'You *are* jealous of me.'

'I'm not. I worry about you—'

She finished her drink and banged the cup down on the table. 'We've been friends for years, and yet the first sign I'm truly enjoying being with someone and you act like this?'

Beth leaned across to touch her arm. 'Wait, stop. I'm sorry. I didn't mean to sound like I'm not glad for you. I am. I just—'

'Just what?'

'Worry that he'll get you in trouble. And would he stand by you if he did?'

'What do you mean?' Katie pulled her arm away.

'He got Lily Johnson doing what you're doing. She started going on trips with him and then doing them on her own. And when she wanted out, as she realised he was using her, Ethan got nasty. She thinks he set her up. She got caught with a large bag of coke that she was taking to Manchester. She's been sent down for twelve months.'

Katie paused. That was the first she'd heard about Lily. Fear coursed through her at the thought of the same thing happening to her. But Ethan told her the first charge thing. Surely, he couldn't be lying?

'I don't know where you heard that Ethan was involved, but you're wrong,' she told Beth. 'He wouldn't do that. He's too nice.'

Beth gasped. 'Will you listen to yourself? A few months ago, you wouldn't have been seen dead with a drug dealer and now you're like his pet dog.'

If Katie hadn't been in a packed coffee shop, she would have slapped Beth across the face. She'd never hit anyone before, but the need to do it now had to be held back. Again, she stared at Beth.

'You're envious, that's all,' she said, eventually. 'Mind you, this conversation will soon be over. It's not as if you are anything to me anymore.'

Beth's eyes brimmed with tears, but Katie continued.

'I thought you were my friend but now I'm not so sure. All this talk of looking out for me? You're jealous of what I have with Ethan.'

Katie watched Beth's face crumble, but she didn't care. She grabbed her bag and stood up to leave. 'When you find true love, I hope you'll know what I'm going through. I adore Ethan, and there is nothing you can do or say to change that.'

Beth called out her name as she walked away, but Katie ignored her. When she was outside on the pavement, she let her anger dissipate with each step she took. She'd always thought Beth was a good friend, but not now. Not when she was jealous of her and Ethan. Because that's what it all boiled down to.

A *true* friend would be happy for her.

CHAPTER FIFTY

Even with everything that had happened over the years, and the illegal business she suspected was being run behind the scenes, Allie enjoyed popping into Kennedy's Boxing Club.

It was late afternoon, so the floor was full of testosterone as young boys and men sparred together, attacked punchbags and generally got rid of their aggression. Females were allowed, too, but only on certain days and at certain times. Steve Kennedy wasn't being sexist when he said they caused too much distraction. Some of the boys to men were indeed quite dishy, even if she did say so herself. She sniggered. If they adopted Poppy, she and Mark would have all this to contend with.

Allie wasn't entirely surprised by Steve's call after he'd witnessed the arrest of Isaac Riley for assault. Only last week, she'd been chatting to Shaun Cooper, DS from the Drug Squad, and if the rumours he was hearing turned out to be good intel, and the Riley brothers were working from the back of the boxing club, Steve Kennedy wouldn't want the likes of them bringing trouble to his door. Not if it meant he'd be breaching his parole. Despite being out of prison, he still needed to be careful. So she was wondering if he might give up Isaac to save himself.

The thud of glove on leather was all around her when she walked through the main area. Steve's office was in the far corner. She passed the rings where two men were sparring to the death by the looks and sounds of the punches. Allie winced when one of them went down to the canvas. It was a brutal sport at times. So competitive. Yet, despite Kennedy's background, it gave the kids something to do and somewhere to be off the streets until nine most evenings, as well as the probable front.

Steve Kennedy was a few years older than Allie. Their paths had crossed on numerous occasions, and she knew she wasn't his biggest fan. So it was equally intriguing for her to get a call from him. He was worried about something. Time to find out.

At his office, she knocked on the door and went in.

'Allie!' Steve cried loudly. It took her by surprise so much that she visibly jumped. Just like the Ryders and the Webbs, overconfident and over-friendly.

'Come on in,' he continued. 'I haven't seen you in a while.'

She smirked. For all his faults and dealings, she quite liked the wit of the man. He was medium build with a superb head of short grey hair, a silver fox some might say. He'd got rid of the pallor from his stretch inside and seemed much healthier than the last time she'd seen him. Being out again suited him, which was why, she mused, surely he'd be worrying about someone as young and stupid as Isaac Riley landing him in strife.

'You wanted to see me?' she said, shifting a pair of boxing pads and then sitting across from him.

'I was a bit concerned to see Isaac Riley arrested and wanted to talk in private to you about the matter.'

'The matter?'

'The reason he was nicked.'

'It's confidential, you know that.'

'I only want to know if it was the girl who was attacked on Sunday evening. The one out with her dog.'

'He's helping with enquiries.'

It was as much as she could, and would, tell him, but it was enough. Steve's face darkened, and she wondered if he might explode at any minute.

'It boils my piss, that sort of thing. I hate violence towards women, as you know. It pains me so much when a man uses a fist to hurt one.'

Despite all his wrongdoings over the years, Allie had yet to hear of him hurting his wife or any other female. She liked how there were certain codes of conduct with criminals, even though anger would be taken out on males. It was all wrong, but she was glad some women got spared.

'How do you know Isaac?'

'He comes in here a few times each week, his brother, too. Isaac has always been the cockier of the two. Ethan is a tad softer and all-round the better one. I don't understand why Isaac would do that to a girl, Chloe, was she called?'

Allie nodded, presuming he'd caught the press release for more details once Perry and Frankie had left for the station with Isaac.

Steve shook his head. 'I wasn't aware they knew each other.'

'She's never been to the boxing club?'

'She was a regular for four months and then she hasn't been in the past five weeks. I checked earlier.'

'How about at Flynn's?'

'Can't say I've seen her, although I'm not in there every evening and we have a lot of clientele.'

Allie paused, gnawing at her bottom lip. 'You've seen the footage of the man running from the scene?'

'Yes.'

'And you think the yellow logo on the hoodie is the same as the Boxing Club's?'

Steve nodded. 'It certainly looks like it, although I wouldn't go on record saying that. The footage is rather blurred.'

'Okay, well, if there's nothing else?'

He paused long enough for Allie to wonder if he was deciding whether to say something.

'No. Thanks for stopping by,' he said eventually.

Allie laughed under her breath. Anyone would think they were the best of pals. It was superficial on both parts. Better to keep the peace until she had more evidence of what he was up to, regardless.

She took one more glance around at the people in the club as she left. Nothing out of the ordinary stood out to her. A couple of the lads glared at her, faces she knew. Two she'd arrested in the past. One she'd put away for six months last year.

Then she drove back to the station to have another chat with Isaac Riley. Charles Dinnen had finally turned up.

It was a disappointing interview. Advised by Mr Dinnen, Isaac had refused to talk to them anymore, and after a weary hour of no comments, Allie had called it a day and bailed him.

Isaac had been told not to go near Chloe Barker, and Allie hoped he took the message seriously. It was up to her team now to get more evidence together over the coming weeks. How she was going to do that was anyone's guess, but she wasn't giving up on Chloe. The CPS needed more than what they had. She wouldn't let her down.

CHAPTER FIFTY-ONE

When Isaac was released, he went straight home. Once there, he slammed the front door in temper. What a day. Not only had he been arrested and bailed pending further, but now he'd taken a call from Steve to say he wanted to see him. Had something gone wrong on one of the lines?

His mum and Ethan were in the kitchen. Isaac ignored his brother's shout and took the stairs two at a time. But Ethan followed regardless.

'Where the fuck have you been?' he asked, barging into his room. 'I've got a message to go and see Steve. He says there's been some trouble. Is this to do with Chloe Barker? Was it you who did her over?'

'I didn't do anything to her.' Isaac thought it best to deny it, even if she said otherwise. It would be her word against his, Dinnen had told him.

Isaac would lie for as long as necessary if there was nothing to place him at the scene. So what if he was running down the road away from her. That didn't mean a thing. 'I don't know what you're talking about.'

Ethan roared and charged at his brother. It took Isaac by surprise when he jumped on his back.

Isaac shrugged him off, losing his balance, and they both fell to the floor. Ethan scrambled over and punched out. Isaac fought back, catching his brother's eye, and then his chin before he could knock him away and get to his feet.

'What the hell is going on up here?' Ruth burst into the room.

'He beat up a girl,' Ethan cried, trying to hit Isaac again. 'Your precious son – he's a loser.'

'You did what?' Ruth's eyes widened and she stared at Isaac in disbelief. 'Is this true?'

'He's wrong,' Isaac said, using his hands to fend off his brother. 'I didn't do anything.' He was on his feet by then. As they stood looking at each other, he lunged at Ethan, cracking him on the jaw.

Ethan came at him again.

'Boys, stop!' Ruth tried to get in between them, but Isaac's fist hit her instead of Ethan. It caught her on the side of her head, and she dropped onto the bed.

Both Ethan and Isaac stopped then.

'I'm sorry, Mum,' Isaac said. 'Are you okay?'

'Yes, yes, I'm fine.' Ruth cupped a hand to her ear. 'But one of you needs to tell me what's going on.'

'Nothing.' Isaac sat down next, rubbing at his chin where Ethan had caught him twice.

'You argue and you bicker all the time, but you rarely go at each other with fists. I want to know what's happened. *Is* this something to do with the girl who was attacked at the weekend?'

Isaac said nothing, so Ruth glanced up at her younger son.

'It's not my story to tell.' Ethan glared at his brother. 'Is it, Isaac?'

'Leave it, I'm warning you.'

'And I'm warning you, Isaac,' Ruth retorted. 'While you're under my roof, you'll behave respectfully to everyone.'

'I didn't do anything! Why don't you believe me?'

'Okay! But if I find out you have and you're lying to me, I'll—'

'This has got nothing to do with you. Either of you.' Isaac got up and pushed past Ethan in his rush to get out of the room.

His mum shouted after him, but he was down the stairs before she could move.

'What is going on?' Ruth looked at Ethan.

'I don't know.' He left and went to his own room, Ruth hot on his heels.

'You were with him on Sunday evening, weren't you? That's when she got attacked, the news said. After she'd been to Katie's vigil and gone home. You were in the pub, weren't you? The two of you?'

'Yeah.' Ethan flopped backwards on his bed. 'He was with me.'

'Well, then why are you so sure it was him?'

'I'm not. He was… so angry that night.'

'But you were with him, at the time she got attacked?'

'I don't know. I wasn't glued to his side.'

'You'd have noticed if he came back dishevelled or covered in blood?'

'He didn't, that's all I know.' Ethan crossed his legs and put a hand behind his head. It was a signal that the conversation was over.

Ruth went downstairs and stood at the kitchen window. The weather was dark, dingy, the clouds grey and almost black in places. They were heading for a storm, in more ways than one.

Then she thought of something. There would probably be blood on Isaac's clothes if he'd attacked that girl. She went back upstairs, into his room, and checked his laundry basket for the hoody he'd been wearing on Sunday.

It wasn't there.

She opened the wardrobe, only to find it hanging up. She lifted a sleeve and pressed it to her nose. It smelt of fabric detergent, and yet she knew she hadn't washed and ironed it that week. Isaac must have done that.

She didn't know what to think now. Was her son responsible for that girl's injuries? Surely not. Then she rubbed her ear again. She'd obviously got in the way when he'd caught her, but there was no mistaking his temper.

CHAPTER FIFTY-TWO

After Isaac was bailed, Allie caught up with her paperwork and then her team. Frankie had given her an update on his visit to Staffordshire College. He'd spoken to a number of students about Katie and Chloe but had drawn a blank with any new intel. Sam had been scrolling through CCTV and door-cam after better images of Running Man. Perry had gone home early to see Lisa and Alfie at his mother-in-law's. So far, he'd drawn a blank with any evidence as to who'd left the items on his doorstep.

She felt bone weary when she let herself into her home that evening. It was half past ten. Poppy would be in bed fast asleep by now. Allie had FaceTimed with her at quarter to eight when she knew she wouldn't get to see her that evening. It was so lovely to have technology available to do that. It almost seemed as if they were in the same room.

Mark was in the kitchen filling the kettle when she went in to him. Dexter came out of his basket to greet her, and she petted him under his chin.

'How's Poppy?'

'She's been grand. You look knackered, though,' Mark

commented, putting the kettle back in its base and flicking it on.

'Charming.'

He winked at her before reaching for two mugs.

She came up behind him and put her hands around his waist. 'It's been a tough day.' Her voice broke a little.

'Want me to help you through it?'

Allie smiled. She kissed him as he turned to her and, now his arms were around her, too, she felt safe. Dealing with the aftermath of Chloe Barker, seeing the photos of the injuries that poor girl had sustained, was a bit too close for her.

Every time she saw images of women who'd been battered and left for someone to find them, she thought of her sister and what it must have been like for her. She'd never known if Karen had been conscious through some of her attack, because Karen had never been able to speak again since that day. Her attacker had ruined not only her sister's life but her parents' and her own.

Fostering Poppy had made Allie more sympathetic to Donna Frost and her family's plight. So she didn't mind if bad memories came to haunt her as it made her more determined to catch Katie's killer.

Chloe Barker had been one of the lucky ones, she mused. Allie didn't see why she would be lying about Isaac beating her up, but it was possible. So she only hoped their evidence was strong enough to give her a good resolution. The girl must be frightened out of her mind that Isaac would come after her again, now that she'd told the police.

The kettle flicked off, and Mark pulled away to make drinks. Allie raided the fridge for a bar of chocolate.

'Want one?' she asked, holding up a KitKat.

He shook his head. 'When was the last time you ate something more substantial than sandwiches or a snack?'

'Probably Friday evening.'

'I'll make you something.'

'It's late, I won't sleep on a heavy stomach.'

'Toast then.'

She shook her head, but when he glared at her, she conceded. 'Okay.'

'Go and sit down and I'll bring it in.'

'Yes, sir.' Allie saluted and, to show she was joking, blew him a kiss and went through to the living room. Before sitting down, she searched out a hardback book that was on a shelf underneath the coffee table. She sat down cross-legged on the settee and opened it up.

It was full of photos of Karen, with her and with her parents. Mark had got it made up into a hardback book for her the Christmas after her sister died. Allie had cried when she'd flicked through it the first time. Every image, memento, and photographed souvenir he could find had been given its own spot, and he'd added words and dates along the way. It had been a beautiful and thoughtful present.

Now, though, as she turned the pages, seeing her and Karen roller-skating when they were ten and fourteen respectively, Karen doing gymnastics on the lawn, and then one of them in fancy dress for school, it was too much to think of what they'd missed. She snapped the book shut.

Mark came into the room with a plate of hot toast with lashings of butter, exactly the way she liked it. Dexter was practically glued to his side, eyes on the prize.

Allie smiled in appreciation when Mark gave her the plate. That was all that mattered now, the future she had with him and a mad dog. And darling Poppy.

CHAPTER FIFTY-THREE

Frankie turned off Botany Bay Road and onto the Birches Head Estate, thankful that he'd be home in a few minutes. He'd messaged Lyla to say he was on his way and had grabbed a takeaway.

The day had been busy, and he was looking forward to seeing his wife. Ben would be in bed now, at this late hour, but he'd catch up with him in the morning.

He drove onto his street, parked his car on the drive, and went into the house. Lyla was in the kitchen when he went through, plonking the bags down on the table. He moved to kiss her before shrugging off his coat and jacket and loosening his tie.

'Heavy day?' Lyla asked, already dishing out the food.

'Long,' he replied, getting two bottles of lager from the fridge. 'Nothing exciting happening, put it that way.' He smiled. 'You know what I mean.'

'You'll find out who did it soon, I have faith in you.'

'I'm glad you do, because sometimes I need to hear that, especially when evidence is thin on the ground. How have you been? Staying vigilant, I hope.'

'Yes, as much as I can. It's hard to keep Ben in, and I worry about being at home alone, but I kept the alarm set on the front and back doors until I saw you arrive a few minutes ago.'

Frankie sat down and dived into his curry. He sighed with bliss after the first mouthful. 'Heaven. I was hoping to get home in time to see Ben, but we had—'

A loud noise sounding like the screech of tyres had them both glancing at each other before an almighty crash, the house reverberating at the force.

'What the hell.' Frankie raced to the front door, followed by Lyla.

They opened it to see a vehicle had driven over their garden and smashed into the driver's side of the car, pushing the front of it into the corner of their attached garage.

Frankie reached for his phone. He was speaking to Control just as the vehicle reversed at force, extricating itself from the metal with a series of face-screwing screeches. Before he could get to the handle, it sped off down the road.

Frankie stood with his hand on his head, relaying the details of the number plate to the operator. 'It's a black Discovery, tinted windows. I couldn't see inside it. Yes, we're fine, but my house and car are not.'

Lyla was standing by his side, clearly in shock, people rushing out to see what had happened.

'Are you okay?' their neighbour across from them shouted. 'I heard such a bang.'

'I'm fine,' Frankie said. 'We're fine.'

'I bet I caught that on my cameras. I'll check it out for you.'

'Thanks.' He turned back to view the damage. 'What a mess.'

'Have they driven off? That's appalling.'

Frankie chatted to his neighbour, but he couldn't help

thinking that he was in the car a few minutes earlier. Had this been a deliberate attempt to injure him or a joyrider leaving the scene of an accident?

'Mum!' Ben cried from behind them.

Frankie and Lyla saw their son in the doorway, looking forlorn in his pyjamas, tears rolling down his face.

'It's okay, love, I'm coming.' Lyla rushed indoors to comfort him.

Frankie waited for the relevant emergency services to arrive. There was going to be one hell of a mess to tidy up. The car would be a write-off, the corner of the garage wall would need to be rebuilt, and new doors attached as those were warped, and the state of the lawn they'd driven over, two tyre tracks gouged into it. Not to mention the For Sale sign that had been smashed to pieces, along with the hopes of an imminent sale.

All superficial, though, nothing that couldn't be replaced. He and his family were safe.

Frankie prayed it would be something and nothing, but he knew better really. He didn't want to put his family at danger due to his job, yet it was par for the course.

So far, he'd been lucky.

TUESDAY - DAY FOUR

CHAPTER FIFTY-FOUR

Going into work the next morning was hard for Frankie. He didn't want to leave his wife or child alone, and yet Lyla insisted she would be okay.

Seeing the damage as it was getting light was terrifying. His car would need to be towed away later that day, a replacement from the garage collected, and then he'd have to purchase another one.

But first he needed to find the bastard who had done this.

He'd asked Sam to pick him up that morning and shared the details with her on the drive into the station.

'It's a bit frightening now, don't you think?' Sam said as she negotiated a roundabout. 'I mean, three of us being targeted, on each consecutive night.'

'Which means Allie will be next?'

Sam gasped. 'I hadn't got as far as thinking of that, even though we mentioned it yesterday.'

'I had. At two a.m. this morning. And three and four and five.'

As soon as he got into the office, he went in to see Allie.

'Hey,' she said. 'I didn't expect to see you in today. How are you?'

'I'm okay, thankfully.'

'And Lyla and Ben? It must have been a terrible shock for you all.'

'Ben was petrified last night, but full of superhero juice this morning. Lyla's putting on a brave face. She's going to be extra careful today. I've told her to contact me about the slightest thing she's worried about.'

'We're all here if she calls. Was there a note left for you?'

'Nothing I can find.'

Sam came over. 'I've checked out the vehicle. It's on false plates. They belong to a white Vauxhall Nova. A couple of people gave statements to uniform, but they didn't really see much. The windows were tinted, so we have no idea who the driver was. But it was found burned out three hours ago.'

'It's another warning, though, isn't it?' Frankie said.

'I'm not sure but I'll take this to Jenny.'

'I've made you coffee, Frankie.' Sam was still hovering in the doorway. 'You seem as if you need it.'

Allie got up to make herself a fresh drink. Perry was at his desk when she returned. 'How are you feeling? Especially after hearing about Frankie?'

'So-so. I'm trying to keep busy and not think about it – which is easy when I'm here. It's two a.m. in the morning when I'm on my own that it gets to me.'

'I can imagine. I've had to move this up the ranks now. I can't contain it at my level. I hope forensics will be able to get us something from your evidence, because what I can't understand is, why now? It can't be connected to this case as it's too organised, but it is a warning.'

'Do you think something would have happened to one of us personally by now if it was, say, Terry Ryder?'

'Possibly, although that could be me this evening.' She feigned mock horror, even though inside she was petrified at the thought. 'Whoever is behind it wants us to realise that they've been watching us to know our home addresses, and also that we're vulnerable because they could strike at any time.'

'Not helping.'

'I know, but like I said to you, our kids can't live in a bubble of "just in case" and neither can we. If every cop who was threatened decided to leave, or not come into work, there wouldn't be a force left. But nevertheless, we can't become complacent.'

'And yet how do we not?'

Yeah.' Allie sighed. 'And now we'll have to trawl through more footage to find out who was driving the car, and its registration details. How are you doing? Did you find anything useful?'

'Nothing yet.'

'Call for you, boss,' Frankie held out the receiver. 'From the desk sergeant.'

'Hey, Robbie, what can I do for you?' Allie sat down next to Frankie. 'Really? Ah, crap. Well, thanks for letting me know. I'll send someone down for a statement. Be about ten minutes.'

Allie gave out a huge sigh when she replaced the receiver. 'Chloe Barker's necklace has been handed in. Apparently, someone found it and took it home. They were going to hand it in but hadn't got round to it. *Apparently,* the press conference jogged their memories. Thieving git.'

'Want me to go and have a word?' Perry offered. 'See where they picked it up?'

'Would you?' Allie hid a yawn. 'I need to get some decent sleep before long or else I'll be good for nothing.'

'Sleep, what's that?'

'We're getting too old for this, aren't we, Perry?'

'Speak for yourself!'

She went back to her office. It was kind of Perry to offer help. It was a DC's job really, but she liked that her team would all do what was necessary without a complaint. Frankie had gone in search of a pool car to go out on site, and Sam had her head down reviewing the rest of the footage coming in from Abigail Matthews's party, and the vicinity of Park Avenue, as well as noting what was coming in on a daily basis.

'Call's come in from a kebab shop on East Street,' Sam shouted over. 'The owner says he recognises the image of Running Man from the press conference. He thinks he was in the shop on Friday evening, late-ish.'

'Excellent. Pass that on to Frankie to check out, please.'

'Will do. Ooh, didn't I always say patience is my virtue?' Sam punched the air. 'I've found footage of Ethan, Isaac, and Jacob dealing at the party.' She peered closer at the screen. 'Nate, as well.'

'Yes!' Allie cried, rushing back. 'So my assumption is they're either selling drugs for Steve Kennedy, or they've thieved some from him to make their own money on the side.'

'They could be passing on takings or making deliveries afterwards, too,' Sam remarked.

Allie agreed. 'It would explain the time difference and why Nate and Jacob are saying they were home earlier than they were, although that is a lot to prove.'

It was a definite possibility, but she'd need search warrants to look for evidence. And was that likely to be in anyone's home or vehicles if they knew the police might be on to them?

'Let's bring them all in. That will be fun seeing Isaac Riley two days on the trot.'

CHAPTER FIFTY-FIVE

Frankie spotted Mo's Place and drove past it, taking a right turn. Smallthorne Road was extremely narrow and busy, so he parked off one of the side roads and walked back. It was a busy little place, a high street for the properties nearby, several shops either side and people milling around on the pavements.

Through one of the large windows, he spotted a man behind the counter at the kebab shop and knocked on the door to get his attention. The man waved, came over, and let him in.

'Mohammed Abir?' Frankie said, stepping inside. 'I'm DC Frankie Higgins. You spoke to my colleague earlier about some footage of someone we'd like to talk to?'

'Mo, yes, come in.' He proffered his hand.

A few minutes later, they were sitting at a table. Mo had a laptop open in front of him. He turned the screen towards Frankie. It gave a view from behind the counter, taking in the inside of the shop and its frontage. Two large glass windows caught the pavement, and a row of cars parked along the kerb.

'Here you go.' Mo clicked a button. 'I'm sure it was this guy. There were a group of them.'

Frankie held his breath for a moment when he saw it was Isaac Riley. Behind him, sitting in the very seats they were in now, was Nate Frost and Jacob Chetwyn. There was no sign of Ethan, which would tally with him dropping Katie off and then going home, he suspected, and the timing was showing later than Nate and Jacob had said.

'I recognised him from what he was wearing but also his build,' Mo went on. 'He's a right cocky gobshite, comes in here a few times a week and always thinks he can boss us around.'

'Sounds about right,' Frankie said, without thinking. He glanced at Mo sheepishly, to find the man unperturbed by the remark. 'Can you send the footage to my phone, please?'

'Happy to help. If it was him who attacked that girl, then he'll be barred the next time I see him. That's not right.'

Frankie nodded in agreement. Suddenly he spotted something. He pointed at the screen, at a car parked close to the door outside. 'Can you zoom in any closer to that vehicle, please?'

'Sure.' Mo clicked a few more buttons, and the vehicle enlarged on the screen.

Frankie could hardly contain himself when he saw someone on the back seat, and he'd seen his face before. He'd been at the vigil on Sunday evening.

The camera footage backed up Isaac's statement, giving them a time of eleven-fifty on Friday night when they left with their orders. Once he sent it to Sam, she could try and plot the route the car took from there to Park Avenue, seeing if there were any drop-offs or anything else that could prove useful.

The group obviously had something to hide, but whether it was related to this case was another matter. And now they could place Nate and Jacob here when they said they were at home, then why were they lying?

Had they been up to no good?

Were they involved in Katie's death and covering up for each other?

And who was the fourth person sitting in the back of Isaac's car?

It was time to dig deeper and find out.

CHAPTER FIFTY-SIX

Hannah Lightwood didn't know what to do with herself. She'd taken the day off to see if she could help Donna and the family with anything. She knew Donna would be suffering in silence, and wanted to be there for her to say that she could rant and scream and cry, or simply talk, and she would be there to listen. But when she'd offered, Donna had said she preferred to be alone.

Hannah wasn't offended in any way. She didn't think the family would have got a minute of privacy since Katie's body had been found on Saturday morning. It must be hell to have their home invaded and the police around every few minutes.

Finally, she used her usual trick to take her mind off things in a crisis. She cleaned.

She bottomed the house and then decided to go up in the loft and root out any things she'd kept from when the children were younger that might come in handy for Shona's baby.

It was quite a task, as once she started opening boxes, all sorts of things came to hand. There were piles of children's books, and albums full of photos – lots with Katie on them because she and Beth had been friends for as long as she and Donna.

Hannah recalled the first time she'd met Donna. They'd started working at the same pottery factory and during their first weeks had been put next to each other. From day one, they'd got on and because they were learning, showing and helping each other, they soon picked up the job. Left together after that, they became inseparable.

Donna was like the sister Hannah never had, so it was sad to see as much as Beth was moping around without Katie, how awful it would be for Donna. She was putting on a brave face for everyone. That was Donna all over. She was the person you could depend on to get you where you wanted to go, with everything you needed, and always with a smile on her face.

Hannah and Wes had been devastated to learn that Max had cancer, and it had been tough for them to watch him go through his illness, deteriorating by the week until he was no more than a skeleton. He and Donna had been such a huge part of their family, their social life, and everything really.

It had taken a lot of getting used to. Wes missed speaking to him on a regular basis, calling him for a chat, or nipping to the pub for a couple at the end of an evening. Hannah missed going out in a foursome. There had always been lots of laughter. At least she still had the memories to cherish.

She paused at a photo of her and Wes, with Beth and Katie sitting on the sofa between them. Wes had been a model for them. His finger and toenails were painted a variety of bright colours, his face plastered in garish makeup, and he sat there as if he was in a family portrait.

Spying what she was looking for, she pulled an old tea chest closer. But then she spotted something familiar that had been shoved out of the way. She reached for it and gasped.

Was that Katie's bag? There had been images of it at every press conference, so she knew it was missing. What was it doing hidden in their loft?

In seconds, her body flew through a range of emotions – fear, shock, angst, disbelief. Then, without thinking, she opened the bag.

The first thing she noticed was Katie's iPhone. It was switched on, although there was minimal battery showing. Hannah's eyes filled with tears when she saw a photo of two laughing teenagers, Beth and Katie's arms around each other. Beth was going to be devastated for a long time, it would be like losing a shadow.

She couldn't get any further than the home screen because she needed a PIN code, and she was glad really because she didn't want to see too much. There could be messages from Katie's killer on there. They could be really nasty or cajoling her, luring Katie to her death.

She shuddered in the silence of the loft. It could only be Mitchell who had put the bag there. Had he attacked Katie for some reason?

Was there something sexual between him and Katie that she had missed – that they'd all missed? Some raging jealousy because Katie thought of him as a little brother and Mitchell wanted more?

Had he come on to her, she'd refused his advances, so he'd hit out at her? He was strong, and capable of overpowering Katie if he was drunk. She'd warned him to be careful as he was going out the door.

Was it simply a stupid accident? She and Wes had taught their son to be respectful to girls and women, to realise when no meant no. Surely he couldn't have tried to force himself on her and lashed out when she'd rejected him?

None of it was corresponding with the sweet, yet cocky, boy she'd sent to school that morning. In his final year and discussing with them what he wanted to do when he left. He said he'd like to be a vet, so he was going on to sixth form. It had surprised her and Wes, and yet they couldn't be prouder.

No, she was being stupid. Oh, she knew Mitchell had his moments, but he wasn't violent, not even to his sister. Sure, they argued a lot, especially being close in age, but they got on well enough.

Hannah ran a hand through her hair. She looked in the bag again. There was a purse with a few notes and a couple of bank cards, a handful of coins, and a bus pass. A recent receipt for a coffee from somewhere in Manchester.

The gloominess of the enclosed space suddenly became claustrophobic, her knees complaining at the length of time she'd been sitting down. Carefully, she made her way downstairs with the bag.

It was still sitting on the kitchen table an hour later.

CHAPTER FIFTY-SEVEN

Ethan parked outside Katie's house. Although a police incident unit was still at the end of the avenue, there wasn't as much of a presence now. Perhaps the things they needed to do had been completed.

He pressed the doorbell before he could change his mind, thankful his dad had given him a few days off after Katie's death. He shoved his hands in his coat pockets, wondering who would open the door. He hoped it wouldn't be Nate or Jacob, or even Shona. Or worse, that copper woman.

It was Donna.

'Ethan?' She frowned. 'Is everything okay?'

'Yes. I hope you don't mind me calling. I... I...'

'Come in.' Donna ushered him through into the kitchen. 'How are you? Have you heard anything new?'

Ethan shook his head. 'I was about to ask you the same.'

'There's nothing yet, but I know the police are working hard to find out what happened.' She pulled out a chair. 'Come, sit. I'll make tea.'

'Not for me, thanks. I don't want to put you out if you have to be somewhere else.' He cursed inwardly. What a stupid thing to say. Her daughter had died, been murdered. 'Sorry, I shouldn't have said that.'

'It's fine. You've missed Nate and Jacob. They've gone to work this morning. Nate needed to do something, he said, to stop him thinking.' She smiled at him kindly. 'We're all grieving and missing Katie, but normality has to go on. I learned that when Katie's dad died. I think he would have liked you.'

Ethan smiled, too, hoping to hide the guilt he was feeling. He shouldn't have come, but he had no choice.

They chatted for a few minutes, and Donna handed him the perfect opportunity to ask what he'd come for when she gave him a photo of him and Katie. It was a selfie. Kate had been obsessed with taking them. He'd played along mostly until he'd got pissed off with so many.

'I thought you might like to have this,' Donna said. 'I've had copies done. It was one of her favourites of you and her. The original was sellotaped to the inside of her wardrobe. It made me cry when I opened the door.'

'Thanks.' He took it from her. 'Actually, I did come for a reason. I gave Katie a teddy bear a couple of months ago and I… would you mind if I kept that as a keepsake, too?'

Donna's eyes brimmed with tears, and she covered her hand with his. 'I wouldn't mind at all, but I think Shona has it. She wanted to keep it to give to the baby, but it's only fair that you have it, though.'

'Oh. No, that's okay.' Ethan swore inwardly. 'I think that's a lovely gesture.'

'Why don't you go and see if there's something else you might like instead?'

Once again, Ethan went upstairs and into Katie's room. He only had a matter of minutes before Donna would come looking for him, so he scanned the room quickly. The teddy hadn't miraculously come back, but he swept his gaze over the room again. Perhaps Katie hid the memory stick somewhere else. It was such a tiny thing to hide that it could be anywhere.

Why hadn't he told her about it? Maybe she could have hidden it somewhere he'd known about then. But he hadn't wanted her to find it. All he'd needed was a hiding place, to keep it outside his house in case Isaac went rooting through his stuff.

Had Donna found it, he wondered? He didn't think so or else she might not have been as nice to him.

What if Jacob had got hold of it? Katie might have found it and given it to him or Nate, even Shona. Maybe with none of them mentioning it, he couldn't be sure.

He searched through as much as he could, but it wouldn't be possible to go through everything.

'It's hard to leave, I suspect.'

Ethan turned to see Donna in the doorway.

'The room,' she said, pointing at it. 'I see her lying asleep in the bed, sitting putting her makeup on, drying her hair. It smells so much of her.'

'I miss her, too.' Ethan picked up the nearest item he could see. It was a compact mirror. 'Could I take this? Would that be okay?'

'Yes, of course.'

'Thank you.'

He left then, glad to be out of the oppressive atmosphere. As he drove off, he banged on the steering wheel. He could only hope Katie had hidden the stick somewhere no one would find it, or she had panicked and got rid of it. He wished now he'd asked her about it, but he'd skirted round the issue purposely. If she'd mentioned it, he was going to say he'd forgotten he'd put it there, or something similar.

Ethan drove home, beside himself with worry. Arriving ten minutes later, he rounded the corner to park in the drive, only to slam on his brakes. There were three police cars outside his house. His face paled, his heart ratcheted up. What was going on now?

The front door opened as he got out of his car. Two uniformed officers were bringing Isaac out of the house. His brother was shouting, giving them grief about the handcuffs they'd snapped on him being too tight.

'Isaac, what's going on?' Ethan shouted.

'They're setting me up, bro,' he said. 'I've been arrested for dealing.'

The blood in Ethan's body rushed to his feet, and then he saw one of the detectives he'd seen on Saturday morning, who'd visited the house to tell them about Katie. Perry, was that his name? When he spotted Ethan, he came over.

'Ethan Lightwood, I'm arresting you on suspicion of dealing and supplying drugs.'

'Hey, wait. You can't do that,' Ruth protested when he was read the rest of his rights.

'We need to talk to them about evidence we've found,' Perry informed her.

'You're taking them both?' Ruth objected.

'It would be better if you waited in the kitchen while we settle them in the cars, Mrs Riley.'

'But this can't be right.'

'They're helping with enquiries at the moment,' Perry finished.

Ethan was led to the car, and he climbed in the back seat. Thankful now that he hadn't got the memory stick on him, he caught his brother's eye in the back of the car across the road. But there was nothing they could say to each other. The police had something on them.

He would have to wait and see what it was.

. . .

Fifteen minutes later, Ruth was sitting at the kitchen table. She hugged herself, wondering where on earth she and Phil had gone wrong. Even without all the stuff with Isaac, she'd known something was amiss for the past few months.

Her boys had changed, and at first she'd put it down to them leaving school, getting jobs and growing up. But it seemed they'd been doing what, dealing drugs? For who, and when? She had so many questions. These boys weren't her children, they were animals.

Maybe the police had got it wrong. Didn't she often say that the youth of today all looked the same – haircuts, clothes, and footwear? It must be a case of mistaken identity.

Ruth remembered how close the boys had been growing up. Since they'd started having girlfriends, and especially since Ethan had been dating Katie, their competitiveness had become worse. They always seemed to be arguing.

But never hitting out at each other. Today had been the worst she'd seen them.

She wondered how long they would be in custody and when she'd be able to get them home again. It was too much to take in on her own, and she was glad Phil was on his way home from work.

When she heard a vehicle outside, she raced to the door and opened it to see him getting out of his car. She rushed straight into his arms and sobbed as if her world had ended right there.

CHAPTER FIFTY-EIGHT

At the station, now all the lads had been hauled in, they'd been put in four different interview rooms on the ground floor. Only Isaac Riley brought representation.

While Perry, Frankie, and Sam chatted to Ethan, Jacob and Nate respectively, Allie went into room one.

'Morning, gents,' she said, pulling out a chair. 'Long time no see, Mr Dinnen.'

Charles raised his eyebrows in a sarcastic nature, and she chuckled inwardly. She could bet he was annoyed to be here twice in two days for Isaac Riley.

Isaac folded his arms and stared at her. He was so alike his brother, except for a tattoo on his right hand of some sort of tribal symbol running from his knuckle to under his jumper.

He was sporting some nasty bruising to his face.

'Been in the wars, have we, Isaac?' Allie asked.

'Ran into a door.'

She smiled sweetly. 'I'd like to ask you a few more questions. You've been here before, so you know how things work. Where were you between eight p.m. on Friday evening and one a.m. on Saturday morning last week?'

'I was out with my mates.'

'Your mates being?'

'Not giving any names.'

'Okay, then where were you with your "mates with no names"?'

'At a party.'

Allie glared at him as he said no more.

Isaac sighed. 'It was at the Bennett Cricket Club, Abbie Matthews's eighteenth.'

'I wouldn't have thought a gig like that would have been your style. I thought you'd have preferred Flynn's.'

It was a dig because they'd picked him up at the nightclub.

'We didn't stay long. It was quite boring but free grub and booze, and a bunch of fit women to have a nosy at was worth a couple of hours of my time.'

'You said we?'

He glanced at Dinnen who nodded. 'I was with Nate and Jacob, as I'm sure you know.'

'What time did you leave?'

'About ten, I think. I wasn't really clock-watching. Didn't think I'd have a need to.'

'What did you do then?'

'Had a ride around, went for a kebab and then went home.'

'Were you in your car?'

'Yeah, because the others don't have wheels like mine.' He pouted. 'They like my Beamer.'

Allie ignored his arrogant tone. She wanted to know more about where he'd been driving.

'Around the area,' Isaac enlightened her. 'It was too cold for walking.'

Dinnen smirked.

Allie ignored that, too.

'So you were at the cricket club from eight until about ten, went for a drive around the area, and had a kebab. Nothing out of the ordinary then?'

'Nope.'

'Did you see Katie Frost at the party?'

'Yeah, she was with my brother.'

'Were they okay, her and Ethan? Having a good time?'

'They were, until that idiot started hassling Katie.'

'What idiot?'

'Tommy Mason. Did he say he was with me? Because he wasn't.'

Allie said nothing. 'We have camera footage of you at the party, photos, too, with a few others. We're still going through it, but we've found evidence of what appears to be you dealing drugs.' Allie showed him one of the video clips Sam had found. There were three young women dancing and looking into the camera. In the background, Isaac could clearly be seen handing something to another teenager in exchange for money.

Isaac sniggered. 'They're sweets I'm sharing.'

'So all the people in this video, and others we have, will say they paid you for sweets when we talk to them?'

'Of course.'

Allie wondered if this was another code to honour.

'Tommy was chatting to her, and Ethan wasn't happy,' Isaac went on.

'Why?'

'She's his woman, and Tommy was getting a little too friendly.'

'Did Ethan and Tommy have words?'

'Not really. But Ethan did tell me he had a go at Katie on the way home and that's why she got out of his car before getting to her house. Sad that, her being so close to home. Have you found out who killed her yet?'

'We're working on several leads.'

Isaac laughed and turned to Dinnen. 'Cop talk for haven't got a clue.'

'So you dropped Jacob and Nate off at home?' Allie went on regardless.

'After we'd been to get kebabs.'

'Where was this?'

'Mo's Place, on Smallthorne bank.'

'Can you confirm what time you left?'

'It was about quarter to twelve.'

'And who was with you? Nate Frost, Jacob Chetwyn, and Tommy Mason?'

'No, Mason left before we did. I think he went home with someone else after having words with Ethan.'

'Was there anyone else in the car?'

'Mitchell Lightwood. He lives near to Nate, so I said he could come home with us.'

Ah, one mystery solved. Frankie would be pleased they'd found out his name. But the plot thickened because Mitchell was the son of Donna's best friends, Hannah and Wes.

'Did you go straight to Park Avenue once you left the kebab shop?'

'I did.'

'And then where did you go?'

'Home. Alone.'

'Was your brother in when you got there?'

'Yeah, it was about half twelve. We had a brew before going to bed.'

Allie knew that could be correct, from what Ruth Riley had said, but she'd been hoping to contradict her. Mothers had been known to cover for their sons in many of her cases, and Ruth couldn't be certain which son had come home at that time as she was in her bedroom.

'Where were you when we called the next morning to update Ethan about Katie's death?'

'At work with my dad, bricking up a wall that had been knocked over.'

That tallied, too, although they would have to get a corroborating statement from Isaac's father.

'Were you shocked to find out what had happened?'

'I was more curious who'd have done it, to be fair,' Isaac said. 'Me and Katie never really saw eye to eye.'

'I heard you were sometimes a nuisance with her.'

'Hearsay, Detective?' Dinnen frowned. 'Really?'

Isaac's face darkened. 'Where did you hear that crap? It must have been that skank of a friend of hers. Or Katie's sister. Shona's known as a snitch.'

Allie wasn't going to tell him. 'Did you ever threaten Katie?' she said instead.

'Of course not.'

Allie glanced at the clock. 'Okay, that's all for now. Let's take a break while I liaise with my colleagues. I'll get someone to bring you a hot drink. I won't be long.'

She went back upstairs, deflated not to have learned much but happy, for now, that even though the boys were lying about something, she had a feeling they weren't involved in Katie's death. The footage showed they were all together at ten minutes to midnight in the kebab house, and even though there were a couple of hours in which the murder took place, she couldn't see them in two places at once, regardless of what time they got home.

So what were they hiding instead?

CHAPTER FIFTY-NINE

Frankie, Perry, and Sam were back from their interviews.

'Anything?' Allie asked them, perching on Perry's desk.

'We were discussing how Jacob and Nate both said they were at home before they were,' Perry told her. 'The footage in the video is clearly them in the kebab shop. What did Isaac say?'

'He dropped them off about quarter past twelve after being in there, which would tally with timing, but not with why Jacob and Nate said they were home earlier than they were. What did they say about the evidence from the party?'

'All three denied it was them in the images,' Sam added. 'And Jacob with Nate visiting Mo's Place at that time.'

Allie rolled her eyes.

'So if they were all together, then surely none are responsible for Katie's murder unless they've covering for each other,' Frankie pondered.

'Katie Frost was murdered between eleven p.m. and one a.m. approximately. So there was enough time for them to go back to Park Avenue and for one of them to attack and kill Katie before they went on their way.' Allie shook her head.

'Somehow, I don't see it. They're all together for most of that time, I admit, but I think they're trying to cover up what they'd been up to by saying Nate and Jacob were in earlier than they were. We need to crack one of them to get to the truth, perhaps scare them a little about the consequences of lying. In the meantime, I'll call Rachel to see if Donna is at home. Because I want to see why she's lying – Shona, too. They both backed Nate and Jacob up. I'm not sure if they're being mysterious for no reason other than panicking or if something else is going on. Either way, if this is wasting our time, I'm going to be furious.'

'It's definitely looking that way,' Perry concurred.

'I hate to say this,' Allie added, 'but I think we need to go back over everything we've done so far and check, check, check to see if we've missed anything. Do the timelines again now we have more details.'

'Shall I go with you, boss?' Frankie volunteered.

'You want to get out of the boring stuff,' Sam protested light-heartedly.

Frankie feigned mock disbelief.

Allie thought for a moment, then nodded. 'Are Nate and Jacob still here?'

'Yes. We were waiting to hear from you before letting them go.'

'Then let's give them a lift home.'

At the Frost home, Allie watched glances shoot between Donna and Nate when she entered the kitchen with him and Jacob. Shona was sitting at the table, her eyes locking with Jacob's.

'Is everything okay?' Donna asked.

'I need to have a word with you all.' Allie pointed to the table.

Chairs were pulled out and sat on in silence. Allie stood at the head of them, Rachel and Frankie either side of her.

'I must inform you that you're all under caution, so anything you say may be given as evidence, do you understand?'

'What's going on?' Donna phrased her previous question another way.

'There seem to be some discrepancies in the timing you got home on the night of Katie's murder, so I thought it best to get you all together. Let's start with you, Nate. Why did you lie about it being at eleven?'

Nate shrugged. 'I was a bit drunk, so I got it wrong.'

'And you Jacob?'

'Yeah, we must have lost track of time, I guess.'

'And Donna, did you lose track of time, too? Why did you say Nate and Jacob were in when they weren't?'

'I-I did think they were in.' Donna eyed the tabletop, her finger following a line in the grain of the wood. 'I thought they were both in bed.'

'At eleven on a Friday night? Was that likely?'

'Jacob had work in the morning, starting at six, so I didn't think anything of it.'

Allie glanced at Jacob, who nodded in agreement.

She paused, then took a moment to stare at each one of them in turn. 'I'm not sure what's going on here, why all the secrecy, but it is concerning me why there are so many lies.'

'We weren't lying,' Donna protested. 'I'm not in a habit of going into bedrooms to see who is home and who isn't. Jacob and Shona are a couple. You wouldn't expect me to check up on them.'

'So what about you, Shona?' Allie's attention fell on the final one in the group. 'Did you conveniently forget everything, too?'

'I... I'm sleeping so much now, what with the baby, so I can't be sure. I'm sorry.'

It was an excuse but one that could be valid. Allie realised she'd been right. It was wasting time sorting this out now.

'This line of enquiry will stay open until we have further details,' she told them. 'I'm not sure what happened in the hours before Katie's death, but if it is to do with any of you, we'll find out sooner than later. I'm sorry to be blunt but I want Katie's killer brought to justice, and I'm sure you do, too.'

They left the house then in another sombre mood. Allie sighed as she and Frankie stood on the pavement.

'What aren't they telling us, Frankie?'

'Do you think it could be linked with dealing drugs on Friday evening?'

'Or who they were dealing for.' Allie nodded profusely. 'I'd take bets on it.'

CHAPTER SIXTY

As soon as Ethan was released from custody, he stormed out of the station. His brother was a few metres behind, but he couldn't bring himself to stop. Ethan didn't want to speak to him and, it seemed, Isaac wasn't keen on chatting either as he lagged behind.

When Ethan glanced again a few seconds later, Isaac was in the distance, walking in the other direction. He flagged down a taxi and clambered into the back.

'Take me to Foxton Street, Kennedy's Boxing Gym.'

All the way there, Ethan wondered if his brother would be heading to the same place. He supposed Isaac might not want to show his face now, in case Steve got wind of either of them being questioned.

But he wanted to square up with the man, offer his apologies before it was too late. Because he and Isaac had fucked up royally at Abbie Matthews's party. Stupid phones! At least the police didn't know about his second one.

He'd checked his own when he'd heard about Katie. All the conversations they'd had were about their relationship. He never talked about work with her unless it was face to face, keeping those details for his secret phone. He knew the police had ways to retrieve information if they found it. Even so, he'd delete anything incriminating once he was home in case they got a search warrant.

Traffic was light, so he was at the club within fifteen minutes. He settled his bill and went inside. It was nearly three p.m., only a few people around before the rush. He knocked on Steve's door.

'Yeah?'

With a deep breath, Ethan went in.

Steve's face was a picture when he saw him. 'You've got a nerve coming here.'

Ethan held up his hands in way of an apology. 'I doubt we'd have got caught if nothing had happened to Katie, but I—'

'Yeah, sorry about that. You were seeing her, right?'

'Now and then, she wasn't anything special.' For some reason, Ethan thought it best to downplay their relationship in front of Steve.

'Nasty stuff, mind. I wonder who it was. Do you have any ideas?'

Ethan shook his head, hoping to change the subject. 'I'll understand if you want me and Isaac out now. We let you down, and I don't want to bring heat to the club.'

Steve sat for a moment, the silence in the room more noticeable when only the sound of glove on glove outside could be heard.

'I think you can continue, for now.'

'Are you sure? I mean, we—'

'I said it's fine. It's your brother who is a liability. You're not responsible for him. Is Isaac with you?'

Ethan shook his head, worried about what Steve had said. In their circles, a liability was someone who needed sorting out. 'We went our separate ways when we came out of the station.'

'Bad blood between you, ay?'

Ethan smirked. 'You could say that.'

'Tell him from me that he's still in the game. You, too. So it's business as usual this evening.' He nodded towards the door. 'Now, scram before I change my mind.'

Ethan turned to leave but spotted Isaac coming towards them.

Isaac sneered when he came into the room. 'What did you tell them?'

'Nothing. I denied it was me in the photos.'

'I said we were giving out sweets.'

Steve roared with laughter. 'And you expect them to believe that?'

'Of course not.' Isaac seemed nonplussed. 'But it's up to them to prove otherwise. They'll need more evidence than that.'

'I wouldn't be too sure.' Steve stood up. 'Now, if you don't mind. I have work to complete before I go home. You two, don't be late this evening.'

Ethan followed his brother outside, noticing his car parked up.

'Thought I'd get it before coming to see Steve. How come you didn't do that?'

'Didn't think. I was so mad.'

'What did you say to him?'

'I told him we hadn't said anything. I wanted to know if he's still okay with us. He seemed fine.'

'Yeah, well, as long as you've kept your mouth shut, then it's all good, bro.' Isaac threw Ethan a look of contempt.

Ethan decided not to answer back.

. . .

Steve sat at his desk, his hands steepled, deep in thought as he watched the Riley brothers through the window until they disappeared from his view. Their body language spoke volumes, Isaac walking like a proud peacock, Ethan following sheepishly behind. The stupid bastards. They were not going to be the undoing of him.

Steve knew it was risky running lines from here, but so far, he'd been kept out of things. Now the police, and that smarmy DS from the drugs team, would be all over him again. He'd have to move the gear before they started sniffing around.

He glanced at the photos standing proud in frames on his desk. There was one of him and his wife and all eight grandchildren on a beach in Tenerife.

Next to it was the whole family at the wedding of his youngest girl, Sadie. He had two further daughters and a son, all together on the steps of the church. Even now he'd been surprised Sadie hadn't wanted to get married with sand between her toes, but she had always been more of a traditionalist.

He'd missed so much of their lives when he'd been locked up. Important dates like birthdays, holidays, the move up to a different school, exam results, and medical appointments. Simple things like sports days, prize-giving, parties, and being the taxi of Dad. Splitting them up when they were scrapping, hugging and teasing them when they weren't.

The last photo at the end of the row was special to him. When he'd got out of prison, Steve and his wife had renewed their marriage vows. Being inside had changed him, and with age he'd mellowed, too. He was so lucky that she'd stood by him. Most women would have given him the boot, but Denise was his childhood sweetheart.

Yet it had been easy to start dabbling again when he came out. A piece of piss not to take advantage.

But he wasn't about to risk being unable to see his family whenever he wanted. It was time to hang up his gloves, and not the boxing ones. Time to quit while he was ahead. Close down the lines, get rid of the evidence.

He knew exactly how to deal with the Riley brothers now. Both of them needed teaching a lesson. No one pulled stupid stunts, or made mistakes, on his watch.

He picked up his phone to call in a favour.

CHAPTER SIXTY-ONE

'What have you been up to?' Shona asked Jacob as soon as they were alone together upstairs. 'You told me you were out thieving on Friday. Are you telling me that you've been dealing?'

'I'm doing it for us, and the baby.' He pointed at the bed. 'Do you think I want to live in a room at your family home forever? We should have our own place, a better car, and money to spoil our girl. I have to provide for you somehow. You know my wage is shit at the factory.'

'I'm not talking about this again, Jacob. You know what I said. If you get my family into trouble or you end up inside yourself, you won't see me for dust. I've lost my dad, and now my sister. I'm not waiting around if I lose you, too. You've brought my family into your dodgy stuff now, and you promised you wouldn't.'

'*I* didn't bring Nate in, Katie did.'

Shona frowned. 'What do you mean?'

'Katie asked Nate if he wanted to get involved because Ethan asked her to. Nate told me about it, and I wanted in.

And you've never said no to any extra money. It's my earner, I can't give up now.'

'I'd swap it all to know that you wouldn't go to prison.'

Jacob sneered at her. 'You say that, but when it comes down to it, I bet you'd think differently.'

Shona gasped. 'I'm not one of your mates you can speak to the hell you like,' she cried. 'I'm your girlfriend, soon to be the mother of your child, and I need you to stop this before you—'

Jacob sliced his hand across her face.

Shona reeled to the side at its force. He came towards her, and she cowered.

He pointed at her, inches away. 'Don't ever tell me what to do. *I* decide what's best for this family, not you.'

Shona said nothing, knowing better than to lip him when he was so angry. She hated this side of him, the ugliness of his moods. But he'd never hit out at her before.

And that changed everything.

'I only want what's best for our daughter,' she managed to say. 'Don't you, too?'

'You knew the score when you got with me.'

She stayed quiet, waiting for his temper to calm so he would leave her alone. She'd got her point across at the very least. And, yes, she had known what he was like when she'd started a relationship with him.

But that didn't mean she couldn't get out of it.

CHAPTER SIXTY-TWO

Friday evening

Katie was surprised to get an invite to Abigail Matthews's eighteenth birthday party, along with Ethan. She wondered if Beth was going, too, but she wouldn't ring to find out.

Even so, she missed Beth. Their friendship had turned sour since the argument in the coffee shop. They'd had tons of rows over the years and usually made up the same day or, at the very latest, the next.

But this time, Katie knew they were done. She was still reeling over the catty things Beth had said about Ethan. Despite what Beth thought, he wasn't only after her for doing the county lines.

The party was a little twee, but they all knew there were plenty of places to deal their wares. Ethan gave her a small bag of pills, and she went off to the ladies', checking out there weren't any olds around.

A group of her friends were gathered around the sink. The three cubicles were empty. She took out a see-through plastic bag and held it high in the air.

'Anyone want a pick-me-up, ladies?'

Eager hands grabbed and parted with money so easily. Katie laughed. It was as if they were a bag of dolly mixtures, and she was already getting known as a face to go to. She liked that.

The door opened behind her. Katie hid the remainder of the drugs in her fisted hand while everyone turned away, intent on doing their makeup. But it was only Chloe Barker. Katie sighed with relief and got back to her sales.

Once done, she checked her own appearance while everyone else left. She heard someone sniffing and turned round. There was no one there, so she listened intently. Someone was crying in the cubicle.

Katie knocked lightly on the door.

'Are you okay in there?'

'Yes.'

'It doesn't sound like it. Wanna talk.'

'Not to you.'

'What do you mean?'

The door opened again. It was Chloe. Her eyes were red, makeup running in tramlines down her face.

'What's wrong?' Katie rushed to put an arm around her.

'It's Isaac. He... I shouldn't be telling you this.'

'I won't say anything,' Katie fibbed. 'I have far more loyalty to the girls than the boys.'

The outer door opened again. Katie pushed Chloe into the cubicle and followed her in. They stayed there while someone had a really long pee. Katie was covering her mouth with her hands, trying not to laugh as it sounded like a horse.

The woman left a few minutes later, and they got back to their chat.

'I don't know how to get out,' Chloe told Katie. 'My mum and dad would go mad if I get a sentence.'

'You won't.'

Chloe looked up at her in astonishment.

'Ethan told me the cops are lenient on first-timers.'

'I don't think that's true anymore.'

'Of course it is. They're not watching for girls. They're after people higher up the chain.'

'I wouldn't be so sure.' Chloe winced and held on to her stomach.

'Are you okay?'

'Yes.'

'Did Isaac hit you?'

Chloe shook her head so much Katie knew she was lying. She thought back to the memory stick that Ethan had hidden in the teddy bear's clothes. She'd seen first-hand what Isaac was capable of when he didn't get his own way. The video was sickening.

'I want out,' Chloe said. 'Isaac has dumped me anyway when I refused to do a run. And yet he won't leave me alone. It's as if I'm his property. As if I can't leave the line.'

As another group of women came into the room, Katie took out her phone. 'Why don't you give me your number and we can keep in touch?'

Chloe got out her mobile and handed it to her. Katie saved her number and gave it back to her. 'Ring me if you need me. I don't like to see you upset.'

She and Chloe left and went their separate ways. Katie found Ethan near to the bar.

'What kept you so long?' he wanted to know.

'I've been talking to Chloe Barker. She's not happy with Isaac.'

'Oh? What's she got to say?'

Ethan's face darkened when Katie told him what they'd discussed.

'She said she wanted out. Why won't Isaac let her?'

'Because once you're involved, you know too much.' Ethan reached for her hand and squeezed it until her fingers were pressed together so much it hurt. He stared at her. 'You do understand that, don't you?' He squeezed harder.

Katie cried out in pain. 'You're hurting me,' she managed to say.

'Let's say I'll do more than that if you mention anything about what we do.'

'I-I would never do that.'

Tommy Mason appeared by her side. 'Everything okay, Katie?' he asked.

Ethan let go of her and stormed off. She rubbed at her fingers, trying desperately not to cry.

'Katie?' Tommy placed a hand on her arm. 'You need to be careful with him. He's dangerous.'

Normally she would have batted off that comment, but the memory stick came to mind. Ethan hadn't mentioned it to her, nor had she said anything to him. Maybe he thought she hadn't noticed it, yet was she wise to keep it now? She knew it was an insurance of some sort, even if it wasn't of Ethan, but it might also get her into trouble.

'I'm fine,' she told Tommy, stepping away from him so that he moved his hand from her arm. If Ethan saw him touching her, he'd go mad.

'No, you're not.' Tommy turned to see Ethan marching back with drinks for him and Katie. 'If you need a lift home rather than leave with him, let me know.' He pointed over to a group of lads at the far end of the bar. 'I'll be over there.'

Ethan drew level with them. 'You still here?' He growled at Tommy.

'Just looking out for a mate,' Tommy replied.

Katie knew instantly he'd said the wrong thing as Ethan passed a drink to her and then clenched a fist.

'I'd leave it at that, if I were you.' Ethan came within an inch of Tommy's face. 'Unless you want to say something to me.'

Tommy held his hands up in surrender. 'I'm going, don't worry.'

Katie watched him return to his friends, half wishing she was going too.

'Is there something going on between you two?' Ethan demanded to know.

'Ugh, no!' Katie laughed to lighten the mood. 'We've known each other since we were kids, and he hangs around with my brother sometimes.'

'Well, he'd better leave you alone.' Ethan took a large gulp of his drink.

'He isn't—' Katie stopped when she saw the sneer Ethan threw her way. But then she thought about the situation. It was wrong what he was saying. It wasn't on, he should trust her.

They stood together for the next few minutes, neither speaking. Before Katie got upset in front of him, she decided she'd leave.

'I'm going home.' She downed the drink and slid the empty glass onto a table. 'Will you take me, or do I need to get a lift off someone else?'

'I'm not done yet,' he replied.

Katie sighed. 'Can't we have some fun rather than work every time we see each other?'

'I have to watch my back. You never know who's out to get you.'

'I've had enough of this.' Katie walked off, but Ethan pulled her back, gripping hard on her arm.

'You'll leave when I say we're going.'

'You don't own me.' Katie did her best to shrug him off.

'Oh, yes I do.' Ethan stared at her, and for the first time since they'd got together, Katie felt uncomfortable in his presence.

CHAPTER SIXTY-THREE

Hannah wept, her head in her hands. It was mid-afternoon, and she couldn't bring herself to do anything about the bag. If it was Mitchell who had harmed Katie, then she needed to know, but she was dreading the fallout.

She hated herself for thinking Mitchell could do anything so heinous, and in some ways, she knew it would be damning to believe that in the first instance without real evidence.

Yet the bag was here because he'd brought it into the house. Whether that was because something had gone wrong when he saw Katie on Friday night, or because he was covering for someone who had asked him to save it, she had to know.

It was hitting her now how much she didn't want her life to be shattered. And how much it was going to be.

She went upstairs and into Mitchell's room, the smell of teenage boy mixed with deodorant and the aftershave he splashed on liberally. It made her sneeze, and she froze, like a thief in the night. She couldn't move, didn't want to know, but she was desperate at the same time to find something to prove Mitchell's innocence.

She glanced around, wondering where to start. The floor was littered with socks, trainers, a pair of jeans squished up as if Mitchell had left them there after wriggling out of them. There were four empty mugs and a small plate in a line on the chest of drawers. His bed was unmade, the covers pushed to the end of it and the bottom sheet ruched where he had slept.

It didn't seem any different than normal. Hannah had battled with him over the years to keep his room tidy but had given up eventually and left him to it. She used to clean it when she was at the end of her tether, when she got sick of seeing the mess, but soon realised this was a ruse because he knew she'd give in eventually and do it for him. For the past few years, it hadn't got better but it hadn't got worse.

He was a typical teenager. And yet she was thinking he would hurt Katie Frost? Hannah idolised her son. She didn't spoil him, but he got away with things that most teenagers would. He'd never brought trouble to their doorstep.

How could she think it was him?

And yet.

She had to know for sure.

Methodically, she started searching through each drawer, then the bedside cabinet and under the bed. She tried to put everything back as it was, so he wouldn't notice she'd been in here.

Sneaking around, checking out his stuff. It felt so wrong. And yet it was so right. A necessary evil.

Next was Mitchell's wardrobe. There wasn't anything untoward with the clothes hanging up, nor on the top shelf. She glanced at the bottom and sighed. Mitchell was a trainer freak – there were so many pairs. She knelt down for ease and reached for the first pair, thrusting her hand inside to find only space. There was nothing inside any of them.

She scurried across the room until her back rested on the

side of the bed, her mind still in overdrive. *Did* Mitchell bring home Katie's bag because he'd attacked her? But if so, why would he do that? He had known Katie for most of his life, and they'd always got on well. There had never been any malice.

Finally, she could wait no longer and called Wes.

'I've found Katie's bag,' she told him, a sob escaping. 'I was looking in the loft for some things to give to Shona, for the baby, and it was there.'

'What?'

'Katie's bag! The one the police are after.'

'The one that's been all over the news?'

'Yes, it's hers.'

'Are you sure? Might it be similar?'

'I'm telling you, it's hers! It has her things inside it, her phone, her purse. Mitchell must have brought it in and –'

'Why would you think it would be Mitchell?'

'Well, it isn't me, or you, and Beth was in all night. Mitchell was out with Nate and that idiot Jacob. You know how I said the family were falling apart. Lord knows what they've dragged him into and –'

'No, I mean, maybe he's keeping it for someone? It doesn't necessarily mean he hurt Katie. He wouldn't do that.'

'Then why is it hidden away out of sight? He knows something. What—'

'Let's think things through a little first. You're saying it has to be Mitchell, but it could just as well have been Beth.'

'She was home and in bed when Katie was killed.'

'Do you know that for certain? Could she have sneaked out?'

'Well, you were home by then. Did you see her?'

'No, I assumed they were both in their rooms until I heard Mitchell coming in.'

'He came in later than he should have from the party at

the cricket club. It was shortly after midnight. I heard him because he was so noisy. It *could* be him. If not, why would her bag be here?'

'It can't be, not our kids. He must be hiding it for someone.' He paused. 'We could get rid of it altogether. If it is either of them, there will be no evidence and—'

'That's against the law!'

'What's the alternative? If we hand the bag in, then Mitchell will probably go to prison. Because whatever has happened must have been something he got himself involved in. He would never hurt anyone like that. Who do you think he might hide the bag for?'

'He has a lot of friends, but so does Beth. It can't –'

'I'm coming home. Sit tight and I'll be with your shortly. Don't call the police until I'm back.'

Hannah put down the phone and stared at the bag. It was no use. After not wanting to do anything for hours, she now needed it out of the house as soon as possible. And she knew the right thing to do.

No matter what the consequences were, Donna was her best friend. She had a right to know, and more than likely there would be vital evidence on that phone.

Finding her mobile, she made a call.

'DI Shenton.'

'I... I... this is Hannah Lightwood, Donna Frost's friend.' Hannah said nothing for a moment, composing herself before she spoke the words she didn't want to. 'I think you'd better come to our house. It's about Katie Frost.'

CHAPTER SIXTY-FOUR

Allie was surprised to take the call from Hannah Lightwood. Her team were all busy, so she rushed over to Park Avenue. Hannah showed her through to the kitchen, in floods of tears and talking so fast that Allie couldn't make sense of what she was saying. She took hold of her arms.

'Stop and take a breath. I can't understand you. Now, tell me slowly this time.'

Hannah pointed at the bag on the table. 'I found this in the loft. It belongs to Katie Frost.'

Allie pulled on latex gloves and brought the bag nearer to her. It certainly looked like the one on Katie's photos.

'Do you know how it got there?' she asked Hannah.

Hannah shook her head. 'It must be Mitchell. He has to be saving it for someone.'

'Could anyone else have hidden it there?'

Hannah shook her head. 'I was home, Beth too. Wes said he came in about eleven.'

'You didn't hear him?'

'No, but only Mitchell was out when... when it happened.'

Allie knew she'd have to tread carefully with Mitchell as

there wasn't enough evidence to say either way what had happened. But she did need to speak to him immediately.'

'Where is he now? At school?'

Hannah nodded. 'He's due back soon.'

'Does he usually go anywhere else once lessons are over?'

'He might stop off at a coffee shop with friends, but mostly he comes straight home and gets changed.'

'I'll have to talk to him. Can you get in touch with him? And perhaps while I'm waiting, I can see his room?'

'Yes, of course. I did a thorough search earlier and didn't find anything else, though.' Hannah reached for her phone and typed out a quick message. A reply came back almost immediately. 'He's nearly here. He's in the high street.'

The front door opened moments later, and Hannah raced out of the room. But it wasn't Mitchell.

'Wes!' she cried. 'The police are here. I couldn't wait until you got back.'

Allie saw the man pale as she watched from the kitchen doorway. 'Mr Lightwood, your wife has found this bag which we believe belongs to Katie Frost. Would you know anything about it?'

'No, I don't understand why it's here.'

'I know you may be concerned for Mitchell, but I'll wait for him to arrive and then take him in for questioning.'

'You're going to arrest him?' Hannah sat down with a thump.

'If there's a simple explanation why he has these items, we can go from there.'

The front door opened again, and Mitchell sauntered in. He frowned when he saw them all.

'Mitchell,' Allie said. 'We've met before, remember? I'd like you to accompany me to the station so we can chat to you about Katie Frost.'

'What about her?' The strap of Mitchell's bag fell from his

shoulder, and he hung it over the bannister. 'Have you found out who killed her?'

'That's what we'd like to speak to you about.'

'Me? Why?'

'If you come with us, we can discuss it at the station.'

'Wait.' Mitchell gasped. 'You don't think I had anything to do with it? I didn't.' He looked at his parents. 'Mum, Dad? What's going on?'

'I don't know, son,' Wes said. 'We'll get to the bottom of this. It's a standard procedure.'

'It'll be okay, Mitchell,' Hannah soothed. 'It's better if they talk to you there. We can get you legal representation if you prefer, and—'

'I don't need legal stuff.' Mitchell shook his head. 'I haven't done anything wrong.'

'Can we come with him?' Wes asked Allie.

'He's a minor so he will need an appropriate adult. We won't keep him any longer than is necessary.'

'You're not going to cuff me, are you?' Mitchell's bottom lip trembled.

'Not if you will go without a fuss.' Allie took out her phone to call for assistance. 'Take it easy and everything will be okay. We'll be in the car and away in a flash.'

A few minutes later, Perry had arrived, along with transport for Mitchell. Wes would have to make his own way there and was already in his car waiting to follow.

As Allie drove back to Bethesda Police Station, something was niggling in her mind, but it wouldn't show itself quite yet.

CHAPTER SIXTY-FIVE

Allie rounded up the immediate team in the incident room.

'Nice break in the case for us.' She popped Katie's bag on the table. Everyone gathered round while she opened it and searched it thoroughly.

'Katie's phone.' She took it out and laid it on the table. 'No battery left on it now but corresponds with the signal bouncing off three towers locally. I was certain we'd eventually find it hidden under a bush that hadn't been searched. I'll get the tech team on to that as soon as.'

Next was Katie's hairbrush, her makeup bag, a bunch of keys, and a notebook. Allie flicked through the notebook first but drew a blank. 'This seems to be about schoolwork.' She looked at Sam. 'Can you...?'

'Yes, of course. I'll do it once we're finished in here.'

'Thanks.' Allie laid everything out and shook the bag to see there was nothing else she'd missed. A pen and a lipstick, a blister pack of painkillers came out of a side pocket.

She tipped out the contents of the makeup bag. 'No necklace in here.' Then she stopped with a frown when she spotted a memory stick. 'This might be interesting.'

Perry opened his laptop, and Allie plugged the stick into it. Frankie and Sam came to stand behind him.

A file came up named ISAAC. Perry opened it and found a video. He clicked on that, too. What came up shocked them all.

Isaac Riley could clearly be seen hitting a young woman in the face and stomach, then grabbing her by the hair and dragging her towards a car. There was no sound, but it was clear she was asking him to stop, her hands around his. Another car came into the car park, and Isaac released her. It enabled her to break free and run back inside. Isaac screeched off in his car seconds later.

'Dear Lord, that's Chloe Barker at Kennedy's Boxing Club.' Allie pointed at the screen. 'She told me about this when I visited her in hospital. Why would Katie have footage of it?'

'Maybe Ethan saw it, took a copy, and gave it to Katie for safekeeping?' Sam suggested.

'It obviously gives him leverage over his brother,' Perry added. 'And with someone like Isaac, I expect Ethan knew it might come in handy.'

'Whatever it was, I'm glad we have it.' Allie sighed. 'We'll have to talk to them both again.'

'They're going to be sick of the sight of us.' Frankie grinned.

Allie did the same. 'Fantastic!'

CHAPTER SIXTY-SIX

Twenty minutes later, nearing five p.m., Allie and Perry went downstairs to speak to Mitchell. He and his father had been shown to interview room three. Wes was sitting next to him, his face as white as a piece of chalk.

She'd spoken to them both earlier about legal advice, but Wes had said that wouldn't be necessary. Allie told him to bear in mind that their conversation could be stopped at any time if he changed his mind.

She set up the recording equipment, stated the time and date, and looked at them both across the desk.

'Mitchell, I need you to tell us in your own words what you were doing, where you were, and who you were with last Friday evening, please. Let's start around eight o'clock.'

'I was at the cricket club, at Abi Matthews's birthday party. I went with Jacob and Nate. Jacob gave me a lift.'

'What happened while you were there?'

'Nothing really. We just had a laugh.'

'There were no fights? No disagreements?'

'Nothing I saw. We hung around at the bar. I'm not

supposed to be drinking but...' Mitchell glanced at Wes. 'I had a bit too much and threw up.'

'I'm sure we've all been there.' Allie smiled kindly. She'd be having a word with the cricket club at a later date, but that wasn't a priority for now. 'What time was that, can you remember?'

'About ten.'

'Did you see Ethan and Isaac Riley?'

Mitchell nodded.

'Did you hang around with them?'

'A little.'

It was as if a switch had turned him off. Mitchell became less responsive the more she questioned him about the Riley brothers. Wes seemed uncomfortable, too.

'So you had a great time with your friends,' she continued. 'How did you get home?'

'Isaac gave me a lift.' Mitchell wouldn't meet Allie's eyes.

'What time was this?'

'Not long after I threw up. We drove round for a bit and then we went for a kebab. After that, Isaac dropped us all off at home.' Mitchell's eyes were watering. 'I didn't do anything to Katie. At least I don't think so.'

'What do you mean by that?'

'I can't remember seeing her after we left the cricket club. I think Ethan was taking her home.'

'Can you recall any of the places Isaac stopped off at?'

'No.'

'Any addresses, or street names?'

Mitchell shook his head. 'He was delivering stuff, I think. He went inside a couple of houses, then came back out and drove to the next.'

'Can you recall exactly how many places you went to?'

'No.'

'And once you'd been to Mo's Place, were all three of you dropped off at the same time, in the same area?'

'Yes, in Park Avenue. Nate and Jacob went in the front way, and I went around the back. I wanted to sneak in quietly if I could.'

Allie couldn't work out then if he was lying or not. If they were all together, then Nate and Jacob would have seen him with the bag. But he said he used the back entrance, supposedly on his own. Was he covering for someone, or was he involved himself?

'Did you see anyone else?' she asked, while she tried to work out the logistics.

'I don't think so, but I can't really remember. I only just made it to the bathroom before puking up again.' He turned his head to Wes. 'You won't tell Mum, will you? She'll never let me out on my own again if she knows I've been drinking.'

'Oh, she knew,' Wes replied. 'We were going to have a word with you about it.' He looked at Allie, eyes pleading for understanding. 'This isn't a regular occurrence. He went to a party and had too much, probably peer pressure. We didn't assume he'd be served as he's underage, but we all know how we managed to get around that when we were younger. He's a good kid.'

Every parent had one of those until they didn't, Allie mused. 'Has anyone else been to your house since Katie died?' she wanted to know from Mitchell.

'I haven't let anyone in.'

'Not Nate or Jacob? Or the Riley brothers?'

'No one.'

'So do you want to tell me now, how did you come to have the bag in your possession?'

'I can't remember much about getting in, but when I woke up, I saw it on my bedroom floor. When I checked inside and saw it was Katie's, I was going to take it back to her. Then when I heard what had happened to her. I panicked and hid it.'

'Why would you do that?'

'Because I couldn't remember if I had hurt her. I can't have, can I, Dad? Did I do something bad because I was drunk?'

Mitchell burst into tears. Allie had no reason to feel they were anything but real. She believed he was telling the truth, because there was still something niggling at her. Something was happening here, a lot closer to home.

'Did everyone in your family get on well with Katie?' she asked next.

'Yeah, I suppose.'

'So no one had fallen out with her? You, your sister, mum or dad?'

'Not that I know of.'

'You didn't know she and Beth weren't talking?'

'No. They do that sometimes.' He glanced up at her through his thick fringe. 'I know I keep on saying, but I swear I didn't do anything to Katie. I liked her. She was funny and kind, and she called me her kid brother.'

Allie had heard enough. Forensic evidence would take a while to come back, but she didn't think Mitchell was lying to them.

Someone else was.

'Okay, Mitchell. I need to talk to my team. I'll get you a cup of tea and a sandwich and I'll be about twenty minutes, okay?' The door opened, and a uniformed officer came in. 'Scott will take care of you.'

Mitchell stood up, Wes following suit.

'Could you stay, Mr Lightwood, please? I'd like a quick word.'

Allie waited until Mitchell had gone and the door was closed again before continuing. She kept the machine running, too. If her theory, what she'd been thinking for the past hour, was right, then Mitchell would be a lot more heartbroken soon.

CHAPTER SIXTY-SEVEN

'Is there anything you'd like to say, Mr Lightwood?' Allie asked. 'Because I'm sure that Mitchell isn't in any more trouble than withholding evidence because he was scared.'

Wes looked at her, pain in his eyes. 'I... I.'

'I must advise you that you're now under caution. If I have to stop the conversation to arrest you, then I will.' She stared at him, unable to stop. 'That's likely to happen, isn't it?'

Wes put his head in his hands.

'Is Mitchell covering for you? Did he see you with the bag, and you threatened to harm him if he told the police about it?'

'No.'

'You hid it in the loft, hoping to get rid of it at a later date, and you told your son to keep it to himself?'

'No.'

There was a long pause, and Allie was about to speak again when Wes did.

'I didn't know he had it.'

'I thought so. So tell me, the couple who were heard arguing, that was you, wasn't it? With Donna?'

'Well, yes and no.'

Before he said anything else, Allie clicked in. Something Donna had done had been playing on her mind. When she'd lied about coming in later than she had, it wasn't only to cover up that Nate and Jacob weren't home. She was covering up for herself, so her family didn't find out what had been going on.

'You and Donna were having an affair,' she said.

'Yes, we were.'

Intrigued as she was about that revelation, Allie had to keep him talking about Katie because she knew her gut feeling was right. 'It wasn't Mitchell who hurt Katie, was it? It was you.'

Allie glanced at Perry from the corner of her eye, to see he'd clearly gathered her chain of thought.

Wes stared at the table, tears pouring down his face, the weight of what he'd done sitting on his shoulders. When he finally spoke, he shook his head in disbelief.

'Yes, it was me. She said she was going to tell everyone and I... I snapped.'

Wes had given Donna a lift back from work. Now they were saying goodnight, sneaking in the back way because she didn't want to be seen with him. But a neighbour had come out with her dog, and even though she'd walked in the opposite direction, they'd moved into the shadows. The whole episode had lasted seconds yet had freaked Donna.

'She wouldn't have seen us,' Wes insisted. 'And if she did, we were doing nothing wrong. I gave you a lift home from work. Where's the harm in that?'

'Because I couldn't lie to Hannah if she found out. I'd go the colour of beetroot, and she'd pry, and I'd give the game away.'

He pulled her into his arms, glad when she didn't resist. 'We have to be careful, I get that. But it pains me not to see you whenever I want. I wake up thinking about you. I go to bed dreaming of you. I don't know what to do about it. I love you, Donna, and I—'

'No.' Donna moved away then. 'I can't do this. It isn't right.'

'Don't be like that. You're spooked, that's all. You have to admit that we're good together.'

'But you're married. To my best friend. And my dead husband was your best friend. You couldn't get any more warped than that.'

'These things happen.' He reached for her again, but she stepped away from him. 'I can't live without you, Donna.'

'What about Hannah? And Beth and Mitchell? What about my kids? It will ruin everything if it gets out.'

'I'm not going to tell anyone.' He smiled and moved closer again.

She pushed him away. 'You don't understand, do you? I can't do this anymore. I have my family to think about, and Shona is due a baby. I can't handle what we're doing. I feel so guilty.'

Wes paused. 'Are you saying you don't want to see me?'

'Yes! No! I don't know.' Donna's shoulders dropped. 'I can't deal with the guilt. What should feel right is so wrong. We both know that.' She turned to leave. 'I have to go in.'

'Wait!' He grabbed her arm. 'Please don't go. I love you, Donna.'

She stayed still for a few seconds, resting a hand on his cheek. 'I can't.'

'Please, Donna. Don't walk away from me!' Although he pleaded, Wes didn't move. He watched her open the gate and then disappear into the house. Then he turned towards the fields, resting his back on the wall, weary with disappointment. He knew what they were doing was wrong, but for him, it felt so right. Hell, he was ready to leave his wife and make things more permanent with Donna. Sod the consequences. She was getting cold feet.

'Oi! I want a word with you.'

Wes glanced to his right and sighed inwardly when he saw Katie.

'What the hell was all that about?' she cried.

He thought it best to deny anything until she'd had her say. 'Oh, hi, Katie.'

'Don't hi, Katie, me. I saw you then, with Mum. You were kissing her. And then I heard her saying she couldn't be with you anymore. Are you having an affair?'

'Would it be so bad if we were?'

'Yes! I mean, you're practically family! I've known you and Hannah all my life. You can't do that to us. My dad would turn in his grave if he could see you. It's sick!'

'It's not like that. Don't be so dramatic.'

'What it is like then?' Katie folded her arms. 'From what I can see you're taking advantage of my mum, and you're married. Have you forgotten that?'

'It's complicated.'

'No, it isn't. It's quite simple really. You stop it right now and I won't say anything to anyone.'

Wes pushed himself off the wall so that he was closer to Katie. She stood her ground, fire in her eyes. He liked her spirit, protecting her mum. But it wasn't going to work.

'I'm not finishing anything,' he said.

'I think you'll find you are.'

'You don't tell me what to do.'

'It's wrong!'

'It's none of your business!'

'I'm warning you. I'll give you until Sunday to finish it or I'm heading right round to your house. I'll tell—'

Wes saw everything flash before his eyes. The life he'd been planning with Donna would be over. He wouldn't be dictated to by a teenager.

'I'm *warning you.*' He pointed a finger in her face. 'Keep out of this.'

'I'll tell Beth first,' Katie went on. 'Won't she be surprised to hear what her dad's been up to? And then, should I tell Mitchell, or your wife?'

The last three words were shouted so loudly that Wes reacted. His hand shot out, and he slapped her.

Katie gasped in disbelief. 'You... you bastard.' She held on to her cheek momentarily, and then came at him.

'Back off!' Wes shoved her hard in the chest.

Katie staggered backwards and lost her footing. Almost as if in slow motion, he watched her go down hard, landing on her back. There was a sickly crack as her head connected with the ground.

She lay still.

'Katie?' Wes said quietly.

There was no response.

'Get up and stop messing around.'

Still she didn't move.

He stepped closer, and it was then he saw the blood, pooling around her ear. Her eyes were open, staring up at the sky. He dropped down to his knees and shook her arm.

'Katie? Katie, are you okay?' Tentatively, he touched her head, moving it to one side, and then his hands went to his own head. Shit, she'd hit the edging stone. There was blood all over it. It must have knocked her out.

He took out his phone to call for an ambulance. But before he dialled 999, he stopped. He couldn't tell anyone he was here. Hannah would want to know why. Donna would crack because Katie was injured. He'd have to move her and say he'd found her somewhere else.

'Katie?' He shook her again. 'Katie, wake up.' He pressed two fingers on her neck to check for a pulse but could feel nothing. He did the same on her wrist. There was no pulse.

Had he killed her?

It was an accident, but he'd go to prison for it.

He could leave her here to be found by someone else. She could have slipped and fallen.

But then, she wouldn't have landed on her back. She'd have probably gone forward. The ground was softer too.

He'd have to move her. If he got her onto the path and hid her in the bushes, it might be blamed on someone she didn't know. No one had seen him with her.

Before he could think things through, he went round to Katie's head and put his arms under hers. He pulled her to standing and then looped an arm around her back to hold her steady.

'Walk with me, Katie,' he said, panic in his voice. But she didn't respond, her head lolling forwards, her hair hanging down so he couldn't see her face.

He drew her nearer, almost off her feet, and staggered with her along the path. When it was too slow, he picked her up and carried her.

At the second set of bushes, he dropped her to the ground, making sure she wasn't too visible. He wanted someone to find her, of course, but not so close to home. Donna couldn't live with seeing her body at the back of her house.

Donna.

He'd killed her daughter.

With no time to dwell, he left. But when he got back to the walkway behind their homes, Katie's bag, which he was going to take with him and destroy in the morning, was gone. He turned around in a circle, thinking it would magically appear.

It wasn't there.

Someone must have found it. Who the hell had walked past? One of the neighbours?

He only hoped it was a thief who had legged off with it and would throw away the contents except for the money. Now he wouldn't be able to get rid of it, switch off her phone.

Now it was all traceable.

With a quick glance round to see there was no one in sight, he ran the few metres along to his own home and slipped in the back gate.

'I never meant to hurt her.' Wes spoke so quietly Allie could barely make out his words.

'Why didn't you get help?' she asked.

'I panicked. I never even thought of her bag until I was running back to the house. I couldn't believe it was missing. I had the shock of my life when Hannah rang me to say she'd found it.' He rubbed a hand over his face. 'What will Donna think of me?'

'I think that's the least of your problems right now,' Allie snapped. 'You've broken not one but two families apart in the cruellest of ways.'

Wes cried again, resting his head on the table, sobbing like a baby. She stared at Perry in disbelief and shook her head. It took all of her willpower not to react. She almost felt as if she despised him. How could he let his son take the blame for what he'd done?

'One more thing,' she said. 'Katie's necklace.'

'I saw it on the ground near her body. It must have come off when I was moving her. So I brought it home. I was going to walk out with Donna, in a few week's time, and drop it on the floor, so she could find it.'

Allie couldn't get her head around that idea. It had stupid written all over it.

'Where is it now?'

'In my toolbox, second shelf down in the garage.'

She left him with the custody sergeant to go down to a cell, while she got Perry to pass details of the case over to the CPS to begin the prosecution. While he was doing that, she'd take Mitchell home and break the news to both families.

She wasn't looking forward to that, but she had to do it. They all deserved to hear it from her.

CHAPTER SIXTY-EIGHT

It was quarter past eight that evening when Allie got back to the station. She'd spent a harrowing hour with the Frost and the Lightwood families. It was so hard to tell everyone what had happened, see their disbelief, then their anger setting in. At one point she'd had to stop Nate rushing round to see Mitchell.

It had been a quiet case, yet even more devastating in ways. Donna had blamed herself for having an affair with Wes. Hannah had blamed herself for not suspecting it was her husband. She was distraught to hear about the affair, but to learn that Wes had killed Katie and covered it up was beyond her comprehension. Allie had sat with her as she'd cried as much as Donna when she'd told her. She truly believed Hannah had no idea about the affair, and seemed to think her marriage was solid.

So many people's lives ruined in one hour.

So it was heartwarming that when she reached her team, they were all smiling. Far more than they should be.

'What's up?' she queried. 'Are you all waiting for curry, because I'm knackered tonight and want—'

'Guess who've been arrested with a car full of drugs and cash?' Perry teased.

She waited with bated breath for them to enlighten her. Although she only needed one guess, really.

'Ethan and Isaac Riley.' Frankie put her out of her misery.

'Oh, that is brilliant news!' She high fived him. 'I needed that to end the day well.'

'Apparently Isaac was shouting that it's all a set up.'

'I might have to agree with him there. It seems a bit... quick and convenient. Not that I'm complaining. It will be great to get them off the streets if we can.' Allie yawned.

'Your day might not be ending that quickly,' Perry added. 'Shaun wants to know if you'll join him for the interview with Ethan. He's struggling to get him to cooperate. Shaun wondered if he might talk to you more.'

'What, because I'm a woman?'

'His exact words he used were a motherly figure.'

'Okay, I suppose that's all right.' Allie beamed. 'Why don't you guys go on home to your families? You deserve a night in with them. Thanks, too, you're such a great team to work with.'

'Whose turn is it for an oatcake breakfast in the morning?' Frankie asked, licking his lips. 'I can taste it already.'

'I'll shout it,' Perry said.

Allie joined DS Cooper in the interview room. Ethan was sitting across from him with a duty solicitor, as pale as Wes Lightwood had been earlier.

'Ethan, I know you're here on a different charge, but I'd like to ask you something. What can you tell me about an attack on a female on the car park at Kennedy's Boxing Club, just before Christmas last year?'

Ethan sank back in his chair, resignation in his posture. 'You have the memory stick.'

Allie nodded. 'We found it inside Katie's bag.'

There was no hesitation from Ethan to explain now. 'Isaac was bragging about what he'd done to Chloe Barker. I knew there was CCTV equipment at the club, so I sneaked in early one afternoon and managed to make a copy of what was on there. When I heard what he'd done to her on Sunday as well, me and Isaac had a row about it because I'd told you he was with me for most of the night and he wasn't.'

'He left you at some point?'

Ethan nodded. 'For about forty-five minutes.'

'So he was all fired up when he got back to the pub?'

'You could say that.'

'Is that why you both then attacked Tommy Mason?'

'I...' Ethan stopped, his eyes closing momentarily. 'Yes,' he said eventually. 'I was mad at him about Friday. He was fawning over Katie, well, at least I thought he was. Katie told me he wasn't, and I would have been fine if nothing had happened to her. But I saw red when he was at the pub after the vigil. I followed him out, and Isaac came, too.'

'Thank you for sharing that, Ethan. Now, are you sure you can't tell my colleague what you know about the drugs and cash found in the car?'

'No comment.'

'Where did you get them from?'

'No comment.'

'Where were you taking them?'

'No comment.'

Shaun sighed.

Allie sat forward to address Ethan. 'Are you saying you don't know, or you won't say?'

'No comment.'

'It's in your best interests to tell us.'

'Look, I'll tell you everything else but that. I will not reveal any names. I can't. I won't.'

'Okay, Ethan,' Shaun spoke then. 'Why don't you start from the beginning and give me what you can?'

Allie remained quiet as she listened.

It seemed Ethan wanted to get a lot off his chest.

When Allie finally went upstairs to her office again, she was drained. The whole day had been a roller coaster of emotions. She could barely keep her eyes open now she could relax a little.

Perry was still seated at his desk when she walked in the main room.

'I thought I told you to head off ages ago,' she protested.

'I had paperwork to do.' He pointed to a pile in front of him.

'Which could have waited.'

'I know.' He grinned. 'How did it go with Ethan?'

'He told us everything but who the supplier was. He dropped Isaac in a lot of stuff, too. He thinks we'll go lenient on him, but you know that's not our call. We can put a word in with the CPS, though.'

'And Isaac?'

'No comment all the way through, even when shown evidence.'

'Will they both be bailed?'

'It's likely. The drugs team found phones on them that we didn't know they had, so there's a lot we have to do before a court case anyway. It's never-ending this job, isn't it?'

'It is. Do you fancy a brew, or even a drink next door?'

'I would love a glass of wine, but I don't think my feet will get me there. Coffee would be nice, though.'

'Coming up.'

She went into her office, hoping not to see a mound of Post-it notes for people she needed to contact. Surprised to see there was only the one, she let her shoulders drop. That could wait until tomorrow.

Perry came in with two steaming mugs as she rooted out a packet of chocolate biscuits. She held them up.

'I only have these.'

'They're dunkable,' Perry said.

'That's not a word.'

'It's good, though.' He chuckled. 'I'm starving.'

'Well, you should have gone home. Is Lisa still at her mum's?'

Perry nodded. 'The house is empty without them. She'll have to come home soon, now the murder is solved. We still have no idea who was responsible, or if they'll strike again.'

'And why do it in the first place? It's a mystery, but something we'll work on alongside our cases.'

They were both quiet for a moment, neither of them wanting to voice that it was likely she'd get some sign that night.

'I'd hate for any of us to suffer when we've put our guard down,' she went on. 'You're all like family to me.'

'Likewise.' Perry paused. 'Except for the youngster. I'd swap him out for someone else in an instant.'

'No, you wouldn't.'

'You're right, I wouldn't. It's fun teasing Frankie, nevertheless. What about you? Are you mithered about what you might find this evening, or in the morning? You're the only one left and—'

'I am concerned, and I have an officer following me home in his car, and the nightshift keeping an eye out when they can drive by. But I'm hoping it will be fine all the same. I don't want Mark to worry too much either.'

'Okay. Let me know when you're home?'

'Yes, Dad.'

They shared a smile of mutual respect. Then they sipped at their drinks while demolishing the biscuits between them. The office was quiet, not a phone ringing. It was bliss.

A message came in from Mark. Allie replied to it, stretched her arms in the air, and yawned loudly. It was definitely time for home.

CHAPTER SIXTY-NINE

After a hearty oatcake breakfast with crispy bacon, cheese, tomatoes, and brown sauce, just the way she liked it, Allie felt refreshed, if somewhat distracted. That morning, she planned to make a few visits, to talk things through with the families and see if they had anything they wanted to know or ask. Once that was done, it would be up to them to work their way through processing everything, with offered support if they required it.

Before she reached Park Avenue, she pulled up in a side road overlooking the pond, glancing over towards the place that Katie's body was found. The crime scene tape had been removed now, and it seemed as if nothing had happened. Except for the fact that several families had been traumatised.

She frowned, peering in the distance. If she wasn't mistaken, there was a pregnant lady sitting on the wooden pier. Rather than head to the Frost family home, Allie took a wander over.

Shona was sitting down, legs out in front, resting back on

her hands. When Allie reached her, Shona moved her head to see who it was.

'Years ago, I'd have taken my socks off and dangled my feet over the side,' she said. 'I wouldn't dream of it now I'm older, and even then, at the moment I'm lucky if I can see my toes, never mind remove my shoes.'

Allie smiled, sitting down beside her. 'Not long now.'

Shona rubbed a hand over her stomach. 'I can't wait to get her out. I want to see that she's okay and hold her in my arms. Do you have any kids?'

'Me and my husband are foster carers. We've had quite a few children to stay over the past two years.'

'Wow, I bet that's hard.'

'It's a challenge at times.'

'Doesn't it hurt when they leave?'

'Sometimes. We've mainly had them stay for a week or two at the most. Some of them we've taken in because a parent or guardian is ill and they go home again once they're better, which could be weeks or months. And then we've had the odd one staying longer.'

'Do you enjoy it?'

Allie looked over the water then as a couple of ducks made a commotion. It had been taxing at times, especially some of the teenage boys. But she and Mark had learned to adapt with every child they'd had to stay. Their first little girl, Amelia, had been the start. She was now settled back with her mum after a three-month battle with an illness had left Amelia needing somewhere safe to be while Mum was in hospital.

'Yes, I do,' she replied. 'When I was younger, I had a sister who died. She was attacked when she was twenty-five. But she didn't die straightaway. She was left in a terrible state and had to live in residential care. She died in 2015. She was forty-four. So, with work, and checking in on Karen, I didn't think I could handle children as well.'

'Do you still miss her?'

'Every day, and always what she could have been. I wonder what she would have been like had she not been attacked.'

'Did you catch who did it?'

'Yes, but it took some time.' Allie shuddered as memories came crashing back to her. The man had hurt her and Mark, but luckily, they'd survived, and he had been sent to prison. 'We got him eventually,' she finished.

Shona smiled faintly. 'I will miss Katie when my daughter is born. I'll miss her through the years, like you did Karen, but I'll always remember every day I had with her. She was my little sister, and I loved her so much. She didn't deserve to die – and not by that bastard. I almost loved him like a father.' She wiped away tears from her face. 'Will that pain go away? I still think about my dad all the time, and I don't know if I have the bandwidth for both.'

'Honestly? It still comes and goes. There are days, weeks, months even, when I don't think of her and then I'll hear a record, or smell something, or see a clip of an old TV programme and it all comes back as if it were yesterday. I suppose that's what you mean about your dad right now?'

Shona nodded.

'You need to grieve for Katie until you get to the same place, and for however long it takes. We're all different in that respect. And never ever apologise to anyone for it.'

They sat in silence for a couple of minutes until Allie stood up. 'I need to see your mum. Are you coming in?' She held out a hand.

Shona reached for it and then shook her head. 'I think I'll stay here a while longer. It's easier.'

Allie laughed. '*I* think I'd want to get that out of me now. I hope everything goes well for the both of you. And that

Jacob sorts himself out, especially now he's going to become a dad.'

'Yeah, me too. I don't fancy taking care of two children.' Shona sniggered. 'Although there might not be a "we" anymore. I had no idea what he and Nate were doing. I don't want to bring a child up into that.'

'Give it time,' Allie advised. 'If he loves you, he should do anything to keep you happy.'

'And if he doesn't?'

'Only you can decide what needs to be done then.'

CHAPTER SEVENTY

'I wanted to call to see how you were,' Allie said to Donna when she opened the door and welcomed her in.

'We're doing okay,' Donna answered. They went into the kitchen. 'We've been through it with Max, and although it's not the same, we do know what to expect. Although Katie was so much younger than her dad, and it doesn't seem real. At least we can get on with arranging the funeral now.'

'Would it be okay if I came along, and other members of my team? I'd like to pay my respects.'

Donna nodded. 'I'll let you know once it's finalised. To be honest, I want it out of the way so I can get on with my life. It sounds harsh, and hard, but I need normality. Would you like a cup of tea?'

Allie chuckled inwardly. It really was the answer to everything.

'I wouldn't say no.' She pulled out a chair and sat down. 'I've just been speaking to Shona. She's by the pond. She seems to be doing well, considering.'

Donna smiled then. 'She is. I can't believe we'll have a

newborn in the house soon. Something to focus all my energy on.'

'I'm glad she has you to help out,' Allie said.

'I'm glad, too, but I'm far too young to be a nan.' She smiled. 'I mean, where did all those years go? Do you have children?'

Allie nodded, happy to talk about the subject again. 'A foster daughter, she's nearly thirteen. My husband and I are hoping to adopt her soon.'

Donna turned to her. 'Oh, that's really nice to hear. I bet it must have been tough, having someone young like Katie being murdered.'

Allie smiled faintly. 'A lot of this job goes home with me, I'm afraid, but I am proud to be a detective.'

'Do you have many unsolved cases, or do you catch most people?'

'We have several outstanding that we're working on. Some are really cold cases, others lukewarm. Often with technology, we find we can analyse an item of evidence with a new piece of equipment and send someone to prison. That's very satisfying. But the majority of cases get solved pretty quickly, even with little evidence as in Katie's murder. They're mostly someone slipping up, often moments of regret.'

'I had no idea it would be Wes.' Donna popped two steaming mugs down on the table and sat opposite Allie. 'Can you imagine trying to blame your own son for something you've done? Why not come clean straightaway? It was a spur-of-the-moment act that went really wrong. Had Katie not mouthed off at Wes – because I'm certain she will have – he might not have hit out.' She smiled, her eyes teary. 'That was Katie all over. And she was mad at Wes for seeing me, maybe that had more to do with her dad than it being Wes and us going behind everyone's back. I regret it now but...' She shrugged. 'I can't take it back and I have to live with the consequences. I wish I could have told you that it was me arguing with him before Katie died. I felt so deceitful. If I had done, he might have confessed earlier.'

'He might not have either,' Allie mused. 'Have you seen anything of Hannah?'

Donna shook her head. 'Our friendship is over. I don't blame her for not wanting to see me anymore.'

'It might blow over eventually. She'll be hurting, too.'

'No. Not only was she my best friend, and I betrayed her, but it's the kids we have to think of. We were always so close, the two families, even when Max died. It's all gone now. We can never get that back. And I didn't have permission to steal her husband because I'd lost my own.'

'We can all do silly things in grief.'

'But if it weren't for me and Wes, Katie would still be alive.'

'You can't haunt yourself with that, Donna.'

Donna was crying openly. 'We never meant to hurt anyone, and we knew it was wrong, but we couldn't stop. And yet I ended up lying to cover up rather than him opening up to what he'd done to Katie.'

'You don't know for sure he would have told you eventually.'

'I know.' Donna wiped at her cheeks. 'Yet I have to live with that. Katie is dead, and it's far worse than feeling sorry for myself because I was screwing Wes for a bit of comfort.' She stopped.

Allie knew she was thinking she'd already said too much, but it was a tragic, senseless accident that should have been handled differently.

They drank their tea, and Donna nipped to the loo. She came downstairs with three black bin liners filled to the brim with clothes. She plonked them on the floor.

'I was taking these to the charity shop. I know it's not

long after Katie's death, but I needed to keep busy and how better than to help others. Katie would have liked that. Maybe your daughter could have a nosy through? Some things might be too big for her, but a lot of them have been hardly worn, and there are some fashionable items, too. I won't be offended if you don't want them, though.'

'On the contrary.' Allie shook her head. 'I used to love having my sister's hand-me-downs. Thank you. Anything she doesn't want, I can pass on to the homeless unit, if that's okay with you?'

'It is. And thank you, too, for everything you've done for me and my family.'

'I'd like to say it was a pleasure, but...'

Both women smiled. At the front door as they said their goodbyes, Allie wasn't surprised when Donna leaned forward and hugged her.

CHAPTER SEVENTY-ONE

After visiting Hannah Lightwood and Ruth Riley, Allie had one more visit that afternoon before she was going home early to spend time with Poppy. She'd missed seeing her these past few evenings and was going to make up for it tonight.

Although she had one thing on her mind, that she'd kept to herself so far. She had received a note that morning. It had been underneath the windscreen wiper of her car, parked on her drive.

Like Perry, she would have to check her door-cam to see if she could recognise who had put it there, see if it was a prank to worry her, or if it might turn into something more sinister.

Like Perry, she was sure there would be no clues as to who it was.

The note had been a simple "watch your back." It was a threat nonetheless, and she wasn't sure what to do about it. She'd deal with it tomorrow work wise, but right now, she wanted to talk to Mark about it first.

Because it had taken her back to 2011, when she'd hidden a note from Mark which she'd received from her sister's killer. He was threatening to come after her next. She'd promised

Mark that she'd never keep anything like that to herself again.

And yet, she didn't want to tell him either.

But she would, and before anyone else.

She pulled into the car park at Kennedy's Boxing Gym. Steve knew she was coming, so she headed straight to his office. He welcomed her in with his usual booming voice, moving things from the chair to give her room to sit down. 'What can I do for you?'

'I wondered if you knew anything about the tip-off we received about Ethan and Isaac Riley, and what we'd find in their possession?'

'I don't have a clue.' Steve shrugged. 'I'm not into that stuff anymore. You know I'm trying to stay out of prison, not get myself sent back. Besides, I've had word that the lines have been closed down.'

'From who?'

'I couldn't possibly tell you.'

They stared at each other. Allie knew he was lying. Steve knew she didn't believe him. But she left it there for now. He'd done them a favour by ending things, and she knew he'd start others up shortly. Once a criminal, always a criminal in her book. The lure of the money would be too much.

She'd bide her time.

'Anything else?'

She opened her mouth to speak about the guarded threats her team had received but changed her mind at the last minute. As much as she'd like his help to find out more, she couldn't trust him.

'I can't think of anything right now,' she said instead.

Steve frowned. 'You're sure about that?'

She nodded and got to her feet. 'Let's hope things stay above board around here, Steve. Family is really important, don't you think? You have so much to look forward to.'

It was Steve's time to nod. 'I do, and I want to enjoy every minute of it.'

Now back in her car, Allie was glad she hadn't confided in Steve about the threats to herself and her team. They would have been forever in his debt, and she couldn't know whether he would go snitching to Terry Ryder. Because the odds were on it being him behind the threats. She had no proof, but now that Katie Frost's murder had been solved, they had time to start digging.

Her concerns around adopting Poppy deepened. She and Mark had spoken about it a lot, and also about fostering further children short term as and when necessary, too. Neither of them wanted Poppy to move on, and after the case she'd dealt with, Allie didn't want to see her go anywhere. She wanted to protect her, too.

Which was why she and Mark would need to have that talk again. If someone was out to get Allie and her team, then it might be better to hang on for a while. See if things settled after this case. Because how could she ensure the child's safety if she couldn't be certain of her own?

Maybe she was too old for this game. At fifty, Allie would love to live a life without fear of retaliation on her team and her family, the people she loved dearly.

Was it time to get a transfer to a safer role in the police? She had some serious thinking to do.

She checked her phone for messages, smiling as she spotted one from Poppy.

Pizza for tea! Will you be home early today? x

Allie typed back a message.

I will, I will. See you soon. x

Great! We have chocolate, too. Oh, and Mark bought your favourite wine ;) x

Allie smiled. Suddenly, her eyes brimmed with tears at the thought of going home to her family.

She thought about Donna, another huge hole in their home.

She thought about Hannah, whose husband was on remand for murder.

She thought about Ruth with her boys and the inability to keep them safe from others, especially from the likes of Steve Kennedy.

Families. Sometimes welcoming, sometimes damaging. Looking after each other. Running from each other. Sticking together. Falling Apart.

Often it was Allie and her team who put them back together again or drove them further away. A small argument turned into a larger crime. A wrong that couldn't be righted. A bond that should never be broken.

Because family mattered.

It was the same with her work colleagues. Some came to try and stifle their good nature, change the dynamics for the better or worse. But her team were always loyal. She wouldn't change a single one right now.

Yes, up until now, she would have said they were all stuck with her.

Allie rushed into the house, not wanting to miss a minute of her time to switch off with her family. Mark and Poppy were in the kitchen, and she smiled when she heard the giggles coming from the room.

'Hey, I'm not too late to join in, am I?' She removed her coat before going into them, Dexter demanding attention by dancing around her feet. 'You know mine will have to have double the amount of mushrooms that you two will put on.'

'Don't worry, I've added a lot to yours.' Poppy pointed at it. 'It's stacked with them.'

'Quite right, too.' Allie grinned. She gave Mark a peck on the cheek and then hid a yawn.

'Everything okay?' he wanted to know, passing her a glass of wine.

'Everything is fine.' Allie took a sip before giving out a sigh of appreciation. She sat down at the island while she watched them finish their masterpieces. There was a strip of red sauce across the back of Poppy's hand.

They were having fun, that was the main thing. Since Poppy had come into their lives, everything seemed perfect. So, for now, Allie was looking forward to some downtime with Mark and Poppy.

When all was said and done, it was family who mattered.

***

First of all, I'd like to say a huge thank you for choosing to read Family Matters. I hope you enjoyed my seventh outing with Allie Shenton and the team.

If you did enjoy Family Matters, I would be grateful if you would leave a small review or a star rating on your Kindle. I'd love to know what you thought. It's always good to hear from you.

Why not join my reader group? I love to keep in touch with my readers, and send a newsletter every few weeks. I also reveal covers, titles and blurbs exclusively to you first.

Join Team Sherratt

ALL BOOKS BY MEL SHERRATT

These books are continually added to so please
Click here for details about all my books on one page

DS Allie Shenton Series

Taunting the Dead

Follow the Leader

Only the Brave

Broken Promises

Hidden Secrets

Twisted Lives

Family Matters

The Estate Series (4 book series)

Somewhere to Hide

Behind a Closed Door

Fighting for Survival

Written in the Scars

Eden Berrisford Crime Dramas (2 book series)

The Girls Next Door

Don't Look Behind You

DS Grace Allendale Series (4 book series)

Hush Hush

Tick Tock

Liar Liar

Good Girl

Standalone Psychological Thrillers

Watching over You

The Lies You Tell

Ten Days

The Life She Wants

Missing Girls

ACKNOWLEDGMENTS

To all my fellow Stokies, my apologies if you don't gel with any of the Stoke references that I've changed throughout the book. Obviously writing about local things such as *The Sentinel* and Hanley Police Station would make it seem a little too close to home, and I wasn't comfortable leaving everything authentic. So, I took a leaf out of Arnold Bennett's 'book' and changed some things slightly. However, there were no oatcakes harmed in the process.

Thanks to my amazing fella, Chris, who looks out for me so that I can do the writing. I wish I could take credit for all the twists in my books but he's actually more devious than I am when it comes down to it – in the nicest possible way. We're a great team – a perfect combination.

Thanks to Alison Niebieszczanski, Caroline Mitchell, Talli Roland, Ed James and Sharon Sant, who give me far more friendship, support and encouragement than I deserve.

Thanks to my amazing early reader team - you know who you are! I'm so blessed to have you on board.

Finally, thanks to all my readers who keep in touch with me via Twitter and Facebook. Your kind words always make me smile – and get out my laptop. Long may it continue.

ABOUT THE AUTHOR

Ever since I can remember, I've been a meddler of words. Born and raised in Stoke-on-Trent, Staffordshire, I used the city as a backdrop for my first novel, TAUNTING THE DEAD, and it went on to be a Kindle #1 bestseller. I couldn't believe my eyes when it became the number 8 UK Kindle KDP bestselling books of 2012.

Since then, I've sold over 2 million books. My writing has come under a few different headings – grit-lit, thriller, whydunnit, police procedural, emotional thriller to name a few. I like writing about fear and emotion – the cause and effect of crime – what makes a character do something. I also like to add a mixture of topics to each book. Working as a housing officer for eight years gave me the background to create a fictional estate with good and bad characters, and they are all perfect for murder and mayhem.

But I'm a romantic at heart and have always wanted to write about characters that are not necessarily involved in the darker side of life. Coffee, cakes and friends are three of my favourite things, hence I write women's fiction under the pen name of Marcie Steele.

All characters and events featured in this publication, other than those clearly in the public domain, are entirely fictitious and any resemblance to any person, organisation, place or thing living or dead, or event or place, is purely coincidental and completely unintentional.

All rights reserved in all media. No part of this book may be reproduced in any form other than that which it was purchased and without the written permission of the author. This e-book is licensed for your personal enjoyment only. No part of this text may be reproduced, transmitted, downloaded, decompiled, reverse engineered, or stored in or introduced into any information storage and retrieval system, in any form or by any means, whether electronic or mechanical, now known or hereinafter invented, without the express written permission of the author.

Family Matters © Mel Sherratt
E-edition published worldwide 2025
Kindle edition Copyright 2022 © Mel Sherratt

Printed in Great Britain
by Amazon